DUDES HARD TARGET

Book Six:

The Dudes Adventure Chronicles

By **Tyler Reynolds**
and **Emily Kay Johnson**

Epic Spiel Press

This work is a work of fiction. Names, characters, places, and incidents are the product of the author's imagination or are used fictitiously. Any resemblance to actual events, locales, or persons, living or dead, is coincidental.

Text copyright © 2021 Emily Kay Johnson

Cover illustration copyright © 2021 Jacquelyn B. Moore

Hardback 2025

All Rights Reserved. In accordance with the U.S. Copyright Act of 1976, the scanning, uploading, and electronic sharing of any part of this book without the permission of the publisher is unlawful piracy and theft of the author's intellectual property.

Thank you for your support of the author's rights.

This book is available in ebook, paperback, and audiobook.

Epic Spiel Press

The Dudes Adventure Chronicles

<u>Save the Dudes</u>
<u>Dudes Take Over</u>
<u>Summer of the Dudes</u>
<u>Dudes in the Middle</u>
<u>Dudes Dog Days</u>
<u>Dudes Hard Target</u>
<u>Dudes Dystopia</u>
<u>The Dude Identity</u>—*coming soon!*

Available in ebook, print, and audiobook
Check them out at: **TheDudesChronicles.com**
Or: **EpicSpielPress.com**

To Wilaya, who will be unassailable.

Contents

Prologue	1
1 Better Homes and Dudes	3
2 Dudes Locked Out	14
3 Dude Deterrence	22
4 Dude Desperado	29
5 Suspicious Dudes	37
6 Dudes Find Loot	46
7 Dudes Empowercd	55
8 Dudes Decoded	64
9 Dudes Arctic Assault	72
10 Dude Delinquent	81
11 Dudes At Home	89
12 Dude Influencers	100
13 Circle Of Dudes	109
14 Re-Dudes, Reuse, Recycle	117
15 Dudes Give and Take	125

16 Dudes Lock Down	136
17 Dudes Upcycle	146
18 Dudes Tank the Neighborhood	155
19 Dudes Make Tracks	163

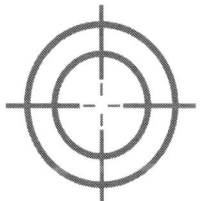

Prologue

Hi. I'm Tyler, and I live in Sherwood Heights. My four best friends are Ryan and Connor Maguire (twins who *don't* look alike but *do* fight a lot), Deven Singh, Nate Howe, and me, Tyler Reynolds. My name is on the cover of this book because I'm the official chronicler of the adventures of the Dudes. (That's what we call ourselves.)

The Dudes love our home town. And we would totally battle to protect it. In fact, one of our biggest problems has always been a lack of real enemies on which to use our awesome battle tactics and superior weapons.

Then, in 7th grade, we got our chance. It turns out that the enemies of Sherwood Heights are not killer robots or zombie hoards or even girls' soccer teams. Actually, they're porch pirates. And that year we Dudes put our energy to work to conquer them. Not only that, but we helped the PTA fortify the school's defenses.

I got it all down on my laptop in The Dudes Adventure Chronicles, and now I'm publishing the stories so the world can know the truth. At some point, I'll probably also write up some parchment scrolls and bury them in a hidden temple, just to be on the safe side. In the meantime, read along and enjoy!

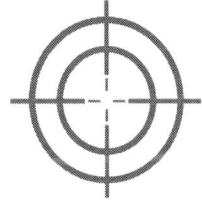

1 Better Homes and Dudes

Last summer was awesome (check it out in <u>Dudes Dog Days</u>), but it couldn't last forever. Summer ended, and, right on cue, the rain started. It wasn't a flood or anything, just the kind of drizzly dampness we always have in the Pacific Northwest in fall.

My family: Mom, Dad, me, my younger brother Jayden, who was 7, and my baby brother Leon, who was 2, were used to this. The difference was, this was my family's first fall to have a dog.

Jayden's dog, Rob, is a collie, so he usually has long hair like this:

Only, over the summer, the Dudes shaved him so he looked like this:

We had found out over the summer that it was really hard to give Rob a bath, so I was hoping the rain would help us out there. But Rob hates getting wet so much that, once the rains started, he avoided going outside. Even when he really had to go, he tried to plod between the drops. So, it clearly wasn't Rob's fault that the whole house smelled like wet dog.

The problem was humidity. Mom's hair frizzed. The windows of Dad's office/shed in the backyard steamed up. And Cheesy Thingies melted if you left the bag open. So, it was only natural that Rob's fur had added a new and fragrant dimension to our home.

Still, nobody was going to do anything about it until one Saturday when we Skyped with Mamaw--my mom's mother--and she said she was booking plane tickets to visit us.

"Great!" said my mom with a cheery smile. But, as she disconnected the Skype, the smile fell right off her face. "We have to get rid of the dog smell!" she said.

"Really?" said Dad hopefully.

"No! I love Rob," protested Jayden.

"Wob-wob!" said Leon, grabbing a woolly clump of Rob's fur.

"Rob's a Dude, Mom," I said, agreeing with my little brothers for once. "We can't get rid of him."

"I didn't mean the dog," said Mom.

Dad gave a disappointed sigh.

"Getting rid of Rob wouldn't change the fact that the carpet smells," Mom pointed out. "No. We'll have to get rid of all the carpeting before Mom's visit."

"What?!" said Dad. "That will cost a fortune. And the new carpet will smell just as bad in a month," he protested.

Mom smiled, like she was way ahead of him. (She usually is.) "Then we'll replace it with hard floors that are easier to keep clean and don't collect smells."

"Well," said Dad, "I suggest you find some wood that is the same color as Rob's fur."

But Mom ignored his advice (as usual) and asked Nate's mom instead. Nate's mom had an opinion on everything, and she was usually right. She agreed with Mom's choice to get hard flooring. (Apparently new carpet outgasses chemicals more harmful, even, than dog smell.)

She recommended this Swedish flooring that was eco-friendly and couldn't be scratched by dog claws. (Scandinavians are apparently way ahead of Americans on that.)

Grandad offered to install the floors for us. He said we shouldn't spend money on a professional just to get it done right. But Mom hired a professional anyway.

He wasn't Swedish, I checked. He came from Ukraine, and his name was Osip. When he came out to do the measuring, he explained that the Swedish floors would be floated in place.

"When will you be flooding the living room?" Ryan wanted to know.

"Yeah, I want to be here for that!" said Connor.

"Floating doesn't have anything to do with liquid," said Osip seriously.

"Is it more of a mag-lev situation?" asked Nate.

"Hmm," said Osip, ignoring Nate as he stared at the spirit level in a long measuring stick he had laid on the floor. The bubble was supposed to sit in the middle of the tube, but I could see that it was way off to one side. Osip moved the stick and squinted at the level again. Now the bubble floated toward the other side.

"Your subfloor has bumps," he finally declared.

"The Dudes could have told you that," I said to Mom. (We did a lot of our hanging out on the floor.)

"Yeah, Mrs. Reynolds," said Ryan. "We figured that's what the carpet was supposed to cover up."

"I'll have to skim it out," Osip said. "Might take more than one layer."

"How *long* will that take?" asked Mom, who had taken off work to talk to Osip, not the Dudes.

"For an area this size, at least a week to skim and dry--maybe longer in this weather," Osip said. "And then there's the installation."

Mom bit her lip. I guessed she was envisioning her mom floating around on the bumpy floors. But she told Osip to do whatever he had to do to fix it.

Osip started yanking up the carpet right away. "You'll need to go to the showroom to choose a color and purchase the flooring," he told her. So Mom got her keys and ran out to the car.

With Osip working in the living room, the Dudes realized that the upstairs would be cut off from the rest of the house. Luckily, the Dudes can adapt to any situation. We started practicing ways to climb out of my bedroom

1 BETTER HOMES AND DUDES

window onto the back deck, then down to the basement door then upstairs to the kitchen.

The new route made getting a snack a lot more exciting. But it didn't work for Rob (dogs not being good climbers), and he was the one who most needed to get out of the house regularly.

When Mom came home from the flooring showroom, she found Ryan standing on a stack of deck chairs, handing tools up to Nate, who was hanging out my window trying to install a pulley system. That's when she decided our family (and the rest of the Dudes, I guess) should move out until Osip was finished with the new floor.

It's not like the Dudes hadn't made a dog elevator before. I told her so while she was packing. But Mom told me that she feared the wet smoothing compound would collect dog hairs and seal the smell permanently into the house.

I thought maybe we would go to a hotel, which would have been cool because there might be a pool. But Mom said that would cost money we didn't have. And Dad said the new floor was already costing money we didn't have. Anyway, Grandad said his RV was like having a hotel in his driveway (which would also be cooler if it had a pool).

And then there was the problem of Leon's potty training. Mom said he needed to sit on his potty chair in a real bathroom every day or he would get confused. Leon didn't actually use his potty chair yet. He just sat on it with his pants and diaper on. Then, when he got up, he got a high five as encouragement. To me, this was already confusing.

Anyway, Mom worked out a system that satisfied her: for the next couple weeks, Mom and Dad and Leon would sleep in Grandad's house (with real bathrooms). Grandad, Jayden, and Rob would stay in the Freewheelin' hotel in Grandad's driveway. And I would stay with Nate (because school was starting and the school bus for Sherwood Middle doesn't go to Grandad's neighborhood.)

My first morning in Nate's house was kinda cool. His family has a totally automated "smart" home. That means his parents have all the interconnected gadgets they can find, and they let Nate do all the programming. At 7am, the blinds on his windows raised themselves, and the sunlight streaming in powered the solar cells on sixteen dancing monkeys (the seventeenth one was being used for something else) that woke us with their wacky music.

After taking my order, Nate pushed the button on a walkie-talkie taped to his bedroom wall. "We'll have eggs for breakfast, Mom," he said.

"Coming right up," said his mom's chipper voice through the speaker.

My mom doesn't like me to tape stuff to the wall, but Nate's parents are all about "indulging his creative engineering instincts" even if it ruins the paint.

The Howes only have one and a half bathrooms, but that wasn't a problem because Nate's family worked with clockwork efficiency. When Nate and I had changed and brushed our teeth, we headed downstairs, passing Mrs.

Howe on the way up in her bathrobe and hair scarf. We found our eggs on the kitchen island and sat on barstools to eat at the counter.

While we were eating, Nate's dad stumbled in, poured himself a cup of coffee from the automated pot, and reached for the refrigerator door. But, suddenly, a video panel on the fridge sprang to life with a picture of a cow X-d out in red. A smooth, simulated voice that I found oddly familiar said:

> Remember to use almond milk in your coffee,

Mr. Howe sighed.

From the pantry, a *ding* sounded, followed by another announcement:

> Your gluten-free rice bagel is ready!

Mr. Howe took the hot bagel from the toaster and set it on a plate. Then he took the plate and his black coffee and went back upstairs to dress.

"Mom has Dad on a lactose free, gluten free diet," Nate told me. "Luckily for us, Mom says a growing body needs exposure to *all* the nutrients, so you and I don't have to be free of anything."

The napkins were cloth, so, when we finished eating, instead of balling them up and shooting baskets into the trash like we do at my house, Nate showed me a toy robot he is programming to refold the napkins to use at the next meal.

First, the wide-spaced arms raised and lowered, fluffing the napkin out flat. Then the robot jerked one arm above the other which resulted in a loose fold.

"Here's where it gets tricky," said Nate. "The robot needs to release this edge and pick it up here to fold again," he said, pointing.

As we watched, the rubber-tipped claws opened and the napkin dropped. The robot moved two inches to the left, then forward two inches, then turned left and knocked over my orange juice.

"Oops. Still working on that program," said Nate, mopping up the spill with the half-folded napkin. He walked to the laundry room and tossed the soggy napkin into a tall canister. The same simulated female voice said:

> A new item has just been added to the laundry hamper. Weight of combined household hampers now equals 76% of a full load.

I realized it sounded like the AI on *Zombie Bash III: Space Station Offensive*, the one that calmly tells you there are no other heartbeats detected in the habitat ring.

"The default voice is customizable to the user," Nate explained. He pointed to the shelf above the sink where a smooth, black cylinder sat. I recognized the glowing blue swirl on the side.

"You have a virtual assistant. What's her name?" I asked.

"It's better not to name them or apply gender pronouns," Nate said, dead serious. "It's a tool, not a person." Nate was the only person I knew who was equally thrilled with and terrified by robots.

Meanwhile, Mrs. Howe jogged barefoot back into the kitchen in yoga pants with her hair pulled into its usual puff at the back and her lips painted a forceful red that matched her toenails.

1 BETTER HOMES AND DUDES

The virtual assistant warned:

> Eight minutes until school transport arrival.

Most people use their smart speakers to play music or order Cheesy Thingies. Some people use them to organize all their other web-connected gadgets. But Nate was a little more creative.

The phone rang, but Mrs. Howe didn't answer. She looked toward the smart speaker. "Play message," she said. A recorded voice came out of the speaker:

> *"I am speaking James from the Internet Computer Service. I have detected a problem with your internet computer device. Call now to give your bank account number and clear up this problem."*

That sounded wrong in so many ways, but Mrs. Howe's lipstick stretched in a wry grin.

"That was too easy, Nate," she said. "It had to be a phishing scheme. No one gets my bank account number--ever!"

"Good job, Mom," said Nate, approvingly.

Mrs. Howe was preparing homemade lunches for us.

"Water on," she told the faucet, and it squirted a bowl of organic strawberries which she divided into two bamboo bento boxes along with veggie sticks and something called tabbouleh.

"Water on," she said again to fill two reusable water bottles and pack everything into an insulated bag.

The phone rang again. This time the message went:

> *"You are in trouble with the Internal Revenue Service. You will be arrested unless you press 9 now."*

Mr. Howe, who was just entering the room, raised his eyebrows. "Like the IRS would ever call you!" he scoffed.

Nate gave his dad a thumbs up. "Good catch, Dad," he said.

> I'll get you next time.

A chill ran down my spine.

Then Nate turned to me. "I've devised a series of tests to keep Mom and Dad on their toes," he explained. "I've heard that older people are susceptible to scams."

"Older than me, honey," said Mrs. Howe.

But Mr. Howe said, "Nate's right. You can't be too careful." He kissed his wife and the top of Nate's head, waved to me, and started toward the garage door.

Before he could leave, the smart speaker spoke again.

> Don't forget your laptop, Henry.

Mr. Howe chuckled, backtracked, and grabbed his computer bag where he'd left it hanging from the stair banister.

> Car is fully charged, airflow to seats started two minutes ago, remember to unplug.

The garage door opened automatically, and the simulated voice called ominously:

> Have a good day, Henry.

1 BETTER HOMES AND DUDES

"I also programmed the route to the office into his car's mapping service," Nate told me. "Sometimes Dad gets angry listening to the news and forgets his turn."

I knew that already. Nate's Dad and mine used to carpool before my dad quit his job to work in our backyard shed.

"Actually," Nate whispered, "the speaker fooled Dad last week and got his credit card number."

"How did it do that?" I asked.

Nate grinned. "It offered to buy him donuts."

> School transport arrival is imminent. Please exit the habitat ring.

"Time to go," said Nate, heading toward the front door.

I hoped I was imagining the cruel edge in the AI's voice as she warned:

> Better take your survival kit. Weather shields are advised.

Nate and I grabbed our backpacks, flipped up our hoods and left for school.

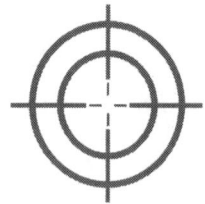

2 Dudes Locked Out

On the school bus, the Dudes usually sat at the back. This served the dual purpose of giving us the bumpiest ride and of separating us as far as possible from Teresa's friends who liked to sit at the front of the bus. (Teresa didn't ride the bus, because she carpooled with her mom, the principal.)

The start of school was hard enough. We didn't want to spend the whole ride being reminded of how the Dudes had been creamed by Teresa's soccer team last summer during the Battle of the Treehouse of Doom.

Of course, Teresa would say that letting it get to us that we were beaten by a bunch of girls just shows how unevolved we are. She says highly evolved people battle each other on the basis of respect, not gender.

"For instance," she told us once. "If Melanie weren't a girl, she would still be my best friend. And, if you weren't boys, you would still be dufuses."

To which Deven had responded, "The joke's on you, because we're Dudes!"

2 DUDES LOCKED OUT

When Teresa wasn't around, Ryan told me: "I respect that they creamed us. I just don't like it."

"And they could do it again if we battle them again," I pointed out.

"Yeah," said Connor. "What we need is a secret weapon!"

"For once I agree with my little brother," Ryan said. "Hey, how come you guys got on the bus together?" he asked.

Nate explained our new living situation.

"Sweet," said Ryan.

When we reached Sherwood Middle School and Mr. Guthrie drove around the bus lane to the back, we saw the other two buses had already arrived and a big crowd of kids was hanging around outside the school doors.

"The doors are locked," Jimmy Dutta told us when we got off.

Ryan pushed his way back onto the bus to ask Mr. Guthrie about it.

"I don't know a thing," said Mr. Guthrie. "I just drive the route. Once you're here, it's up to the school to let you in."

"Can you drive us home to ask our parents about it?" Ryan tried.

"Not until 3:00," said Mr. Guthrie.

So Ryan and the Dudes pushed our way to the front of the crowd and peered in through the glass doors. The lobby was empty, but we could see through the lobby to the glass doors at the front of the school. The front door is the one you enter if you walk or if your parents drive you to school. I could see there was a pile of kids peering in there too.

"It appears all the doors are locked," said Nate.

"Maybe there's no school!" hoped Deven.

"Look! Someone's coming," said Connor. "It's Mr. Swenson."

I cupped my hands around my face and saw Mr. Swenson, the custodian, walking out of the 6th grade wing with a recycle bin in his hand. When he saw the crowd at our door, he dropped the bin and started to rush over, pulling his keyring out of his pocket. Then the kids at the door on the far side must have knocked because he stopped, turned, and took a step toward them.

The bus kids started knocking and pressing pleading faces against the glass. But the other side was doing it too. Mr. Swenson turned his head to look at one door then the other, fingering his keys. Finally, he shrugged and crossed the empty lobby toward the office.

"Ugh!" the crowd groaned. It wasn't cold, but Nate's AI had been right about the rain, and we were all getting pretty wet.

"Mrs. Gutierrez is coming!" said someone, as our principal marched out of the office in blocky heels and a pantsuit. Mr. Swenson followed along meekly behind her. She directed him toward the front door, and Mrs. G used her own key to unlock the door to the bus lane.

As the door opened, so did Ryan's mouth.

"No questions, Mr. Maguire," said the principal, cutting him off. "Proceed immediately to homeroom for some important instructions."

We were seventh graders now, but the Dudes had the same homeroom teacher this year as last year--Mr. Isaak. Nate's mom had explained that the plan is for students to have one teacher who stays with them all three years of middle school to develop a deeper relationship with the students. Mr. Isaak didn't seem any happier about it than we were. But then, he never seems happy.

"Students will please take a seat and listen carefully," said Mr. Isaak grimly. "I am now passing out student cardkeys," he said, handing me a white plastic card with a picture of a salmon on one side and a black stripe on the other.

"From now on, you will use these keys to enter the building in the mornings," the teacher went on. "When everyone has their cardkeys, we will devote today's homeroom time to a question and answer session."

Connor raised his hand right away. "Do we still have to take 6th grade social studies from you?" he asked.

Mr. Isaak rolled his eyes. "You are in 7th grade now, so you should refrain, as much as possible, from asking stupid questions."

Ryan raised his hand next. "I don't think these cards are going to work," he warned. "I tried opening a locked door with a credit card one time, and my mom still hasn't forgiven me for breaking her Warehouse Store card."

"The administration has anticipated this question," said Mr. Isaak, darkly. "Students will please direct your attention to the video on *proper* use of your cardkeys."

Mr. Isaak turned on the active board and showed a Youtube video of happy people sliding their cards down a slot, waiting for a green light, and then opening the door to the rhythm of a bouncy tune.

Soon, though, the music plunged into scary, dark chords as a guy without a card tried shaking the handle, but the plucky door wouldn't open for him.

When the next woman turned her card salmon-side up, she got a red light and some whiny-sounding music. Only when she had turned the card over did she get a green light and a trumpet fanfare as she entered the building. She winked and nodded in appreciation of what she'd learned.

Mr. Isaak turned off the screen before a singing hamster clip could begin. "I assume you have absorbed the video's message," he said.

Nate raised his hand. "I appreciated the cinematography," he said, "but the soundtrack was overblown." (Nate was almost as passionate about moviemaking as he was about robots.)

Mr Isaak rolled his eyes and said, "Students are to remember the phrase: Slide, Green, Open."

Gina raised her hand. "Will this card give us access to the senior patio?" she asked.

Mr. Isaak shook his head. "Only 8th graders can access the senior patio, for which they use their ID's not their cardkeys."

"Are 8th graders at least locked out of the rest of the school?" asked Connor.

"All students will have access to the school," intoned Mr. Isaak.

"But we *always* had access to the school," said Nate.

"Now the school doors will be locked at all times," said Mr. Isaak. He didn't sound happy to be locked in with us.

"You mean they were unlocked before?" asked Ryan. "Like at night and on weekends?"

"Definitely not," declared Nate. "I've gone back loads of times to try to get my lunch box or my oboe when I forgot it, and I couldn't get in. Wait, will this let me *in* on weekends now?"

Mr. Isaak sighed and looked at his watch. "Students will still be unable to access the school when school is not in session," he said.

Ryan frowned. "How do they work that if we have these keys?" he asked.

"Your cardkeys won't work when the school is locked," said the teacher. "They will only work when the school is unlocked."

"You mean when it's *open*, but it's *still* locked," Nate corrected.

Mr. Isaak sighed and nodded.

"What's the point of locking school when it's open and we're supposed to go inside?" asked Deven.

Teresa sounded like she actually knew what was going on. She probably did, since she was Mrs. Gutierrez's daughter. "They're not protecting the school from the *students*," she said.

Mr. Isaak looked like he thought they should be, but he said mournfully, "That is correct."

Ryan was pleased with the arrangement. "We all get keys to the school? Awesome!" he said.

Connor agreed. "This will totally fix that problem of Mr. Swenson and Mrs. Gutierrez having to let us in," he said.

Mr. Isaak checked the bottom of his mug for more coffee.

Teresa's friend, Melanie, brought up a new concern. "What about my dad when he picks me up for orthodontist appointments in the middle of the day?" she asked, poking at her braces with her tongue.

"Or my mom when she comes to volunteer?" added Nate. "Do PTA members get keys too?"

Mr. Isaak shook his head. "There is a doorbell and video camera at the front entrance," he explained. "You may tell your parents to ring the bell and wait for the office staff to identify and buzz them in."

Nate saw this as a security weakness, of course. "If they're going to buzz them in, what's the point of locking the door?"

"The locks are not meant to protect the school from parents," said Mr. Isaak.

"So, what kind of an invasion are we expecting here?" asked Ryan, clutching his pencil like it was an F-S commando knife. I know he didn't listen to the news or anything, so he probably figured there might be a war going on he hadn't heard about yet.

"The locks are for our protection," said Mr. Isaak vaguely.

"He means they're to prevent an active shooter getting into the building and, you know, actively shooting us," said Nate (who *does* listen to the news, plus, his mom's the head of the PTA's new Security Council).

A couple people gasped, and kids started glancing toward the door.

"But couldn't they just shoot us through the windows?" asked Deven.

"Not if they were bullet-proof glass," said Connor.

"Bullet-proof glass is very expensive," Nate pointed out. "Usually, only governments and criminals can afford it--not schools."

Now kids were glancing at the windows.

"The shooter won't be outside, anyway," said Ryan. "They'll be coming from the hall, after Mrs. Ritter buzzes them in."

"She won't buzz in bad guys," argued Teresa. "She'll call the police."

"What if my dad looks like a bad guy?" worried Melanie. "He shaved his head, and he's kinda got this Russian mafia thing going on. He thinks it's cool," she explained.

"I don't think Mrs. Ritter has to worry about trying to decide," I pointed out. "Bad guys probably won't ring the doorbell. They'll just shoot out the glass and walk in."

"Or maybe they'll get frustrated with the whole cardkey thing and shoot themselves," said Deven.

"Gross," said Teresa.

"The cardkeys are meant to make us feel safer," said Mr. Isaak dryly. "Further questions may be directed to the district administration or to the PTA, who paid for the security measures."

He heaved a sigh as the bell rang. "Students should now proceed to their first period class," said Mr. Isaak.

"See you tomorrow, Mr. Isaak," called Ryan. "Good talk."

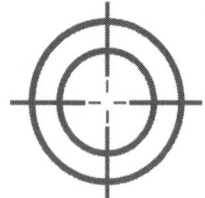

3 Dude Deterrence

Dudes were used to thinking about enemies and watching out for attacks. Ryan was totally confident that we could fend off any attack the school could offer. But that wasn't true for everyone. Somehow, getting told we were so secure had raised a lot of kids' insecurities--or maybe created some they hadn't had before. Go figure.

Even I had a nightmare that week about a big guy who kept coming no matter how many times I shot him. He was really scary, and he had a soccer ball for a head. Come to think of it, that nightmare could have been about our battle against Teresa's soccer team.

Anyway, it woke me up, so I used the faint light of Nate's TARDIS nightlight to quietly make my way to the hall bathroom. Unfortunately, when I turned on the light, wacky music began to play. I had forgotten there was a solar powered dancing monkey hanging over the toilet tank. I quickly grabbed the monkey before it could trigger the electric eye auto-flush. Then I turned off the light and did my business in the dark.

The newly locked school doors didn't just cause nightmares. They caused problems in the daytime too. For instance, in P.E. we had to go outside for flag football. But nobody could carry their cardkeys because the P.E. shorts don't have pockets.

The boys' teacher, Coach Gregor, a walking mountain of a man, solved that problem. He rolled his battered old roller chair from his office to the gym. While the girls' teacher, Coach Rachel, took us all out for brisk exercise in the fresh air, he made it his job to sag into the chair and wait inside the door. That way the gym was protected, and he was available to let kids in and out to the bathroom.

Once we were outside, Coach Rachel explained that flag-football is like real football except without the tackling. But most of our class didn't know the rules to real football. Coach Rachel was supposed to explain them to us, but she only got as far as the "first down" before she turned sort of green and said, "Why don't you just start playing and learn as you go."

I figured this was her way of avoiding all the questions that usually slow things down like: "Why do they call it football when you can use your hands?" and "Is there flag-soccer?" and "Why do we have to exercise?"

Anyway, our version of flag-football turned into a game of tag, where we all wore flags and ran around trying to grab them. (And, of course, Ryan and Connor still tackled each other.)

"First down!" shouted Deven as Ryan hit the turf.

While we were standing around, watching the wrestling match, Melanie said nervously, "Now that we've locked them out, how do we know the crazy people with guns won't be waiting out *here* when we come out for P.E.?"

"I *hope* they are!" said Ryan, wrapping the flag he'd just taken off Connor around his fingers like a garotte. He narrowed his eyes and looked around.

There was no one on the field but a bunch of lazy seventh-graders. Even Coach Rachel didn't look as peppy as she usually did. She was slumping on the bleachers with circles under her eyes. I wondered if she had nightmares too.

"There is nothing to worry about outside," Nate assured us.

"Right," Deven put in. "The outside is everywhere, and we don't have to have cardkeys for everywhere, so it must be safe!"

I was still going over that statement in my head when Nate said, "I looked up some statistics. Most active shooters are students or former students," he explained reassuringly. "So, reason would suggest that they are likely to have a cardkey which would enable them to do their shooting inside."

"That's a relief," said Melanie.

But Ryan kept an eagle eye while we were outside, just in case someone decided to target the tennis courts or something.

P.E. wasn't the only issue. The whole security thing had highlighted the basic inequality in our society. As Nate pointed out: "In a system that relies on people carrying their cardkeys and using them correctly, the lazy, immature, and irresponsible are bound to get disproportionately bad results."

And it was true. By the end of school that week, a bunch of people had already lost their cards or left them in their lockers or at least had wasted precious chat time searching a purse or backpack. I felt lucky to still have my cardkey in my jeans pocket by the time the bus dropped us off at Nate's house Friday afternoon.

In the kitchen, Mrs. Howe was preparing what Nate called her "power purse". That afternoon, she was going to another meeting of the PTA Security Council. (It's probably pretty much like the one the President of the United States has. I imagined her at a long table in a room plastered with screens, examining threat assessments from around the globe.) Apparently, they weren't done securing the schools yet.

"Students need to be empowered to take charge of their own safety," she said, pressing her lips on a folded tissue and then dropping her lipstick tube into her bag. She added breath mints, her tablet in a neon pink Black Lives Matter case, aluminum water bottle, protein bar, wet wipes, mini first aid kit, nail clippers and hair ties. She slid mirrored sunglasses into a side pocket and attached a dispenser of hand sanitizer to the strap. Other than the hair ties and lipstick, it was pretty much what she puts in Nate's backpack only prettier.

"I left you some snacks to help with your homework," she said as she checked her phone.

"Thanks, Mom...oops," I said. "I mean, Mrs. Howe," I corrected.

The mistake was embarrassing, but Nate's mom seemed pleased. She smiled and squeezed my shoulders as she breezed out of the house, pouf bobbing.

Nate told me that his mom had planned to have only one child on whom to focus all her mothering. "But she seems to have underestimated her energy potential," he explained. "Now she's trying to spread the mothering around, I guess."

I nodded. It probably explained the whole Security Council thing too. I know my mom didn't have time to focus on three kids *and* security.

Nate and I didn't have homework. The teachers probably figured learning to use the cardkeys was about all seventh-graders could handle this week. So, we carried the snacks to Nate's room and used our time wisely, working on new ideas for scam tests.

"In 2020, $79.9 million was reported lost in fraud schemes involving gift cards," Nate told me. "They are a popular payment method for scammers."

Mr. Howe was still at work, so we were the only ones home when, unexpectedly, the toilet flushed and we heard wacky music coming from the hall bathroom.

I was even more surprised when Nate shouted: "That's the proximity alarm!" and shot out of his seat.

Nate had set up a motion-sensor at the edge of the driveway. Someone pulling-in had triggered a dog-barking app from a bluetooth speaker he had mounted just

3 DUDE DETERRENCE

inside the front door. The sudden sound then triggered a clap-activated light switch for the stairs and upstairs hallway. The lights coming on were what had triggered the monkey in the bathroom. The monkey's wacky flailing then caused the hands-free toilet to flush by itself.

Nate's bedroom is on the back of the house, but, this way, he got advance notice when someone was coming to the door. (We all had to brush our teeth in the dark, and Mr Singh kept complaining about the Howes' noisy dog. But that was a small price to pay for security.)

"I bet it's the Dudes," I said as we raced downstairs.

"Let's see how my new Verbal Security System handles them," said Nate.

"Verbal Security System?" I repeated.

"I have a theory that words can be a cheap, safe, and effective means of deterring intruders."

He took out his phone, which buzzed at the same time the doorbell rang.

"Mom bought one of those video doorbell cameras," he said. "The ad said it would defeat porch pirates."

"What are porch pirates?" I asked.

"It's another name for package thieves. The claims are bogus anyway," Nate complained. "The cameras don't prevent anything. They just take a video." Nate clicked the link on his phone. "I made a few enhancements to ours," he told me.

On the screen, we could see a young man in a brown shirt and shorts carrying a package. As he reached the porch, I heard a deep, gravelly, but familiar voice say:

> You have entered the maximum security zone. It is in your best interest to adopt a

> **harmless posture and to name and display all weaponry.**

The young man gripped the package in front of his chest. The video was high def. I could see his Adam's apple bobbing as he swallowed.

The voice said:

> **You have fifteen seconds to state your justification for being in the security zone.**

"Uh, I have a package?" said the young man nervously. There was a pause while the delivery guy sweated.

Then the voice replied sternly:

> **You may proceed. But keep your hands visible.**

On Nate's phone, I saw the delivery guy drop the package, back off of the front step, and run back to his truck.

"That was the voice of Judge Grimm from *Space Police*, right?" I asked, as we heard the delivery truck rev its motor and speed away.

"Yeah," said Nate. "It probably wouldn't have worked near as well on the Dudes."

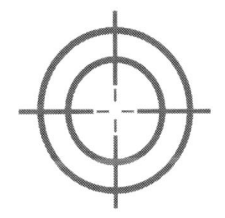

4 Dude Desperado

A week later, I was finally allowed to go to my own home after school. Nate's house had been great, but I was anxious to see what the new floors were like. Of course, the Dudes came with me.

We were bummed to find that Osip's team had already moved all the furniture back from where it had been piled in the garage all week. The stacks of furniture would have been a great place to have a dart gun battle. Instead, we found Mom's side of the garage empty (because she had taken her car to work), and the other side filled up with Dad's car. So, he must be working in his shed/office.

There was a sign at the door telling us to leave our shoes in the mudroom. I guess we were going to become one of those houses where you take off your shoes before you walk inside.

"It's more hygienic," said Nate. "It's commonplace in Japan and Russia."

"It's commonplace here when your grandmother is coming to visit," I told him.

Since the middle school gets out earlier than the elementary, I was surprised to find Jayden already at home. He was playing The Floor Is Lava by hopping from one piece of furniture to another to avoid touching his bare feet to the cold hard floor. (Which is kind of the opposite of lava, but, okay.)

"Hey, little Dude," said Ryan.

"I'm not little, obviously," Jayden scoffed as he leaped from the couch to the coffee table.

The Dudes took in the changes. "The room looks bigger," I said.

"The ceiling should be roughly two inches farther from the floor with the carpet removed," Nate pointed out.

"It would look even bigger without furniture," said Deven. (Another thing the Dudes had planned to do was play wall-ball in the living room.)

"Let's see if it echoes," said Connor. He went to the kitchen and brought back nacho flavor Crunch Balls for sound testing. The Dudes and Jayden gathered around the dining table. The crunches did sound a little louder than usual, but you couldn't hear it with the crunches in your own mouth, so we had to alternate chewing.

When it was my turn to listen, I heard Rob whining on the other side of the sliding door. I went to let him in from the deck. He walked right in, his nails clicking on the new floors, crossed the room, and collapsed under the dining room table. He seemed to like lying on the lava. Besides that, he gave us something warm to put our feet on while we ate our snack.

Connor and Deven tried playing finger soccer with a crunch ball, but Deven had an advantage because the balls tended to roll toward his goal.

"Leveling the floor seems to have revealed the tilt of the table," Nate pointed out.

That wasn't the only unfortunate surprise that day. It turned out that Jayden was home because of what my family later took to calling The Pizza-Gun Incident.

It started when Jayden was in the cafeteria eating his school lunch and he made a pizza gun.

"How did you do that, Jayden?" I asked.

"Ooh! Where is it? You could use me for target practice," offered Connor. "I'm still hungry after the Nacho Balls."

"The gun doesn't shoot pizzas, obviously," said Jayden. (He'd started saying "obviously" a lot, obviously.) He sighed and then explained it to us. "You know how the pizza at school is square?"

"Just one of the many ways school food is weird," said Deven.

"I ate my pizza until it looked like a gun," Jayden explained.

"I can see how that would happen," said Ryan.

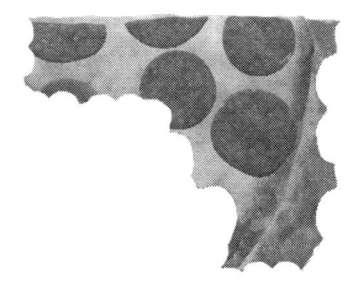

"Then Mrs. Boehner, the lunch lady, said I should eat my whole lunch," Jayden went on. "But I said I couldn't because then Marcus would shoot me with his carrots."

"That's just good defensive strategy!" said Ryan clapping him on the back.

"It might be possible to shoot pizza *rolls*," Nate mused. His imagination had been captured by the engineering challenge. "They are projectile-shaped."

"Anyway," Jayden went on, "when the bell rang, Mrs. Boehner took me and the pizza to the principal's office. And Mrs. Brandenmeyer said I wasn't supposed to make weapons at school. Then they called Dad."

"And you picked him up?!" asked Mom, outraged, when she heard the story later after the Dudes had left.

Dad shrugged. "What am I *supposed* to do when they call me to pick up my son?" he asked.

"You should defend him!" said Mom. "They took food away from our child."

"Jayden did say he wasn't going to eat his gun," I pointed out to defend Dad.

"I wasn't that worried about it," Dad said. "What are they going to do, give him a bad grade in lunch?"

"I'm gonna get a zero," said Jayden seriously. "Mrs. Brandenmeyer said they had a zero policy on weapons."

"They are branding our son a violent troublemaker," Mom complained. "He was probably just eating the green pepper parts first because they are his least favorite," she said, smoothing Jayden's hair with her fingers. "You know he always does that."

"Uh, sure," said Dad like he actually pays attention during meals.

"It's as much their fault as his," Mom went on, "making food that looks like a weapon in the first place."

"Gosh, Mom, it all looks like guns," I pointed out, "Carrot sticks, burritos, hot dogs..."

"I guess making a gun out of *pizza* was actually pretty creative," said Dad.

"That's the problem with our culture," said Mom, turning on all of America now. "We're so focused on violence that every red-blooded American boy sees guns everywhere."

The rest of Mom's tirade was drowned out by Leon's yelling.

"Yah-yah-yah-yah!" he shouted over the sound of stamping his shoes. Of course, he had his shoes off his *feet* like everybody else. But Leon had brought his shoes from the mudroom and was now crawling with the shoes on his *hands*, whacking them against the Swedish finish as hard as he could. I would have liked to point out that at least he wasn't using them as guns, but no one could have heard me.

The noise effectively stopped Mom and Dad's argument, which, I guess, was another benefit of the Swedish finish. The brochure hadn't pointed out how loud it could be. (It was all about how it couldn't be scuffed up or dented--which is what had sold Mom. She didn't want the floors to end up like our furniture.)

Anyway, Mom stopped arguing with Dad and emailed the principal of Jayden's school. She said it was wrong to blame Jayden when he felt he had to defend himself (she didn't say against carrots).

But the principal passed along the email to the school counselor, who might have got the wrong idea, because, the next day, there was another email. In this one, the school counselor said she would be happy to help if Jayden wanted to report any episodes of bullying.

"What's bullying?" asked Jayden when Dad read out the email to us that afternoon.

"Everyone knows what bullying is," said Dad. "It's like when a big guy scares you into giving up your milk money," he explained.

"What's milk money?" asked Jayden.

"Is it anything like Coconut Bucks?" I asked.

Dad sighed and turned off his Bluetooth headset. "I mean the money you have to pay to get your milk at school," he said.

"Don't *you* pay for our milk?" I asked. "Isn't that why they're always sending those robocalls that our lunch accounts are getting low?"

"Yes, but, when I was a kid, we had to bring cash and pay it to the teacher," Dad said.

"So she'd like you?" asked Jayden.

"No, it was for the milk," Dad explained.

"Did you lose your meal card, Dad?" asked Jayden. I thought he was beginning to feel some sympathy for poor, bullied Dad. Dad probably should have leaned into it, but instead he said, "We didn't have meal cards back then."

"Why not? Was it the olden days?" asked Jayden.

"It was because we didn't have computers," said Dad, which should have answered Jayden's question right there.

"Was that because you spent your money on milk?" asked Jayden.

"No. Nobody had computers when I was a child," Dad explained. "I've told you that before."

"It *is* pretty hard to believe, Dad," I told him.

"How did you play Minecraft in the olden days?" Jayden asked.

"I think we're getting a little off topic, here," Dad complained. "The point is I had to bring money for milk and a bully might try to take it."

"Like those guys who call and say you'll go to jail unless you buy them a gift card!" I said, remembering Nate's scam statistics. If they all grew up without computers, it's no wonder the older generation was so easily fooled.

"Good thing we don't have to pay for milk anymore," said Jayden.

"Of course, we have to pay for milk," said Dad. "Son, don't you know how your meal card works? Your mom and I pay money to the school, and then they post it to your computer account and the card is used to subtract it when you buy a meal?"

"I shouldn't have to do subtraction at lunch," argued Jayden. "It's my break."

"That's not the point," said Dad. He looked for a second like he didn't remember what the point was. Then he said, "Your meal card represents money."

"Really?" said Jayden like he'd never thought about this before. "Can I use it to buy online games?"

Dad sighed, said "no", and turned his Bluetooth back on.

I figured Jayden was safe from bullies anyway. After all, he seemed pretty creative at making weapons.

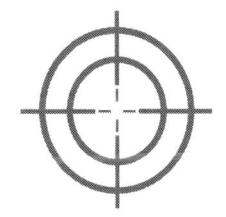

5 Suspicious Dudes

The school building was now a hard target. Which mostly meant it was hard for students to use it. For a while I suspected the whole thing was a ploy to promote niceness at school. (They do that all the time. The adults call it Social/Emotional Learning.) After all, the way they had set things up, they created a group of students (the absent-minded or disorganized ones) who were disadvantaged when it came to getting into the school. Helping one of them, therefore, was an everyday good deed.

And it was true. For about a week Sherwood Middle was a kinder, gentler school with everyone holding doors for the person behind them or running over to open doors for people who had gotten accidentally locked out. Every kid was thinking *it could be me next time.* It was a glimpse of a better world.

Then came the crack down! Who would have thought we could be using the doors wrong--especially after all those how-to videos. But it turns out the PTA Security

Council didn't *want* us to be nice. In fact, as Teresa explained it, being nice was contrary to the goal of being safe.

"You'll feel safer if you imagine the person behind you is evil and has a gun," she explained, which is just the kind of crazy thing that only Teresa can say convincingly. Of course, she said this through the glass while refusing to open the door for Nate when he couldn't find his cardkey.

Bus students who forgot their cardkey had to go all the way around the school to the front door. Once there, we had to ring the doorbell for Ms Ritter, the school secretary, to let us in. This represented the school's first line of defense.

I guess it was a lot of pressure because Ms Ritter was getting pretty snippy about all the people coming late and ringing her doorbell while she was trying to do stuff like her job. She'd read you the riot act while she wrote you a late pass for class--which was embarrassing in front of all the other kids who were also waiting around for their passes. (There was usually quite a crowd.)

Leave it to Ryan to figure out a better way. He started keeping his books in a paper grocery sack.

"You ring the doorbell and then hold the bag in front of your face when the camera comes on," he explained. "Just use your deepest voice and say 'I'm here to make a snack donation for the health room.' Ms Ritter always buzzes in PTA parents who are doing their duty," he said. Once you were in, it was easy to sneak past while Ms Ritter was writing hall passes for less enterprising kids.

"But what happens when you get to Mr. Isaak's class?" I asked. I knew he wouldn't fall for that grocery sack routine.

Ryan shrugged. "I'm inside the school by then. And I don't have a late pass, so I must have been on time. Why would he question it?"

(It was true. Mr. Isaak just rolled his eyes and told Ryan to sit down.)

Nate says that's an example of what's called "social engineering". It basically means how easy it is to get around security because of how people aren't robots. (Which he thinks is what's wrong with the world.)

Nate had found a workaround too, accidentally. After Teresa wouldn't let him in, he had picked up his backpack and headed around the building toward the front. While he walked, as usual, he was thinking about something else--in this case, a way to hack the security system and open the doors with his phone.

I guess he was pretty distracted by the time he got to the back side of the cafeteria and found the kitchen doors propped open. (In fact, the kitchen doors are often propped open because of the sauna-like conditions created when 250 pounds of frozen tater tots get warmed up for lunch.)

Nate walked in without noticing. The kitchen staff paid him no attention either--because he wasn't a tater tot, I guess. A few minutes later, he found himself in the 7th grade hall, so he shrugged and walked in to homeroom.

Under Mr. Isaak's steely glare, he reported truthfully, "Sorry for being late. I had to dump out my backpack to look for my cardkey." (Of course, he failed to mention he hadn't found it.)

"Fine," said Mr. Isaak glumly, waving Nate to his seat behind Ryan.

The empty seat next to him was Connor's.

It turned out Connor had also run afoul of Teresa. Only he had circled the opposite way around the school and, on the way, found an open window on the ground floor. It was the classroom of a seventh-grade social studies teacher, Ms. Bak. Luckily, we were on the Ancient Civilizations unit, and she had brought a Chinese screen and some bamboo plants in pots to decorate the classroom and set the mood.

Like a ninja, Connor climbed through the window into the space behind the screen where no one could see him. Ms. Bak was standing at the active board showing the How to Use Your Cardkey film again. (It was an instant classic.)

While her back was turned, he crept from the screen to behind her desk. But Ms Bak was standing between him and the door. Connor realized he was trapped. At any moment, she might step behind her desk and find him.

Luckily, about that time, some late students came strolling down the hall, chatting loudly.

Ms Bak walked toward the door to shush them. And, while her back was turned, Connor stood up, walked quietly to the nearest empty desk, and sat down, hoping to blend in with the others of his kind.

When the teacher turned around her eyes lit on Connor in the front row, started to pass on, and then returned, pausing on Connor's face. Even though he wasn't in her homeroom, Connor had her for fourth period, so he probably looked familiar.

The other kids weren't reacting to Connor's presence. Homeroom is a time that a lot of kids use for getting more important things done, like finishing their homework, texting their friends, or checking on the release time of the new *Space Police* update.

Connor himself would have normally been digging into his emergency snack pocket. But, today, he was frozen under Ms Bak's confused stare. He saw her eyes narrow slightly and her lips purse as if there was something she wanted to say...

Then, like the sound of freedom, the bell suddenly rang and homeroom was over. Ms Bak's eyes moved to the planner on her desk.

Connor took the opportunity to stand up and walk out with the rest of the class, breathing a sigh of relief on the way to first period. (Luckily, Mr. Isaak hadn't reported him missing from homeroom--probably because he didn't want him found.)

You can see how finding work-arounds gave the Dudes something interesting to keep our minds occupied at school. I had been pretty lucky so far. The new security measures didn't get me until Thursday.

Because our school is overcrowded, my Spanish class is in a portable building. It looks like a trailer on the outside, but inside it looks like a room--kind of like Grandad's RV, but less comfortable. It has carpet and walls and a ceiling (which puts it ahead of the Dudes' dojo, come to think of it). But, unlike Grandad's RV, it doesn't have a bathroom. So, on Thursday, during third period, I had to take the *baño* pass and walk past the tennis courts to the main school building.

It was only as I reached the front doors that I remembered the school would be locked. I didn't have my cardkey, which was still safe in the headphones pouch of my *mochila* in the *edificio portatil*.

I hesitated on the sidewalk. I felt kinda embarrassed about asking Ms Ritter to let me in to use the bathroom. Of course, it would be even more embarrassing to wet my pants.

I decided to walk around to the kitchen. But, for some reason, the doors weren't propped open today. I tried to look in, but the little window in the door was steamed.

Then, as I turned around, I saw a bunch of slumping kids in shorts shambling out toward the soccer field. P.E.! I wasn't wearing shorts, but I bet Coach Gregor would let me in without a word (he pretty much did everything without a word).

So I started across the senior patio (which was deserted this early in the day) toward the back of the gym. That's when I suddenly heard a voice behind me.

"Hold it right there!" the voice said.

For a second I imagined Teresa's evil guy with a gun.

But I turned around to see Officer Racarro of the Sherwood Police. (The Dudes had run into him on a few occasions, some of which he knew about.) Since he was a cop, I guess he was tough. But he was Sherwood's youngest cop. Being a middle school student, I knew lots of adults who were more evil than him.

He didn't even have his gun. (He later told me the PTA Security Council wanted a policeman on campus, but Officer Morgan had said it was a bad idea to carry a gun when you were going to be around kids. I wasn't sure how to take either of those pieces of information.)

5 SUSPICIOUS DUDES   43

"Why are you out here?" Racarro asked. "Is it passing period or something?" he added, glancing around. "I lost track of the bells," he admitted.

Then he squinted at me. "I know you, don't I?" he asked.

I relaxed and said hello.

It turned out Racarro was the new school Resource Officer. I thought that meant he was here to guard the school supplies and hand sanitizer--you know, resources. But he told me his job was actually to *be* a resource for the school. So far, that meant harassing sweltering kitchen workers and kids out of class.

Luckily, he had a cardkey. When I showed him my *baño* pass, he let me in to use the restroom so I could finally go back to Spanish class in time to say *adios*.

Later that afternoon, Ms. Gutierrez introduced Officer Racarro to the whole school at the See Something/Say Something Assembly in the gym. Apparently, if we *see something* suspicious, Officer Racarro is the guy we're supposed to *say something* to.

The assembly was pretty weird. First, Principal Gutierrez talked about how we had to protect each other by being strong and unified and creating solidarity within the school. Then Ms. Howe took the mike as president of the PTA Security Council. She told us how we had to be suspicious of everyone and prepared for attack.

Luckily for Racarro, the Resource Officer didn't have to speak. After the assembly, we all lined up to get an official police high-five.

(High fives are powerful. Mom's using them at home to potty-train Leon. Just for the promise of a high five, he's willing to sit on his potty seat 8 times a day for two minutes each. Of course, four of those times, he's at Grandad's house. I've noticed all the adults get really excited whenever they do a high five with Leon. They smile with teeth and scary big eyes. And Grandad even pretends the slap hurt his hand, which makes Leon laugh. Of course, Leon is just a toddler and impressionable. Soon enough, he'll get wise and demand candy or money like the rest of us.)

Officer Racarro didn't just offer high fives. He gave everyone magnets that featured a smiling Sherwood Steelhead with the words "'Sea' Something/Say Something", which, I guess was better than a high five and nothing.

"You don't have to guard the Dudes," Ryan told him. "We like to take care of our own security."

We were supposed to put the magnets on our lockers. But, because our school was overcrowded, lockers were optional. Nate had one to store his Oboe, and Connor had one to store extra food in case of an emergency (like a snack attack, I guess). But three out of five Dudes just carried everything on their backs and hobbled from class to class like Quasimodo. (The Hunchback of Notre Dame is an awesome book, by the way, and has nothing to do with football.)

Anyway, it was the end of the day. So, everybody put the magnets in their pockets or purses or backpacks--basically the same places that they also kept their card keys.

Did you know that the black stripe on security cards is magnetic? The next morning, we found this out when lots of kids showed up to school with their cardkeys wiped by their See Something/Say Something magnets.

Ironically, it was less of a problem for the absent-minded and irresponsible kids who had lost their magnets or slapped them on teachers' cars. It was the sharp kids, like Teresa, who had put their magnets in a safe place next to their cardkey and now had no way to get in the school.

Of course, Nate, who had forgotten his cardkey yesterday and who had already lost his magnet became the hero when he showed up with a working card the next morning and used it to open the door for Officer Racarro and then for all the other kids

All except Teresa, of course. Good thing she wasn't actually hiding a weapon in that neon pink purse, because the Dudes could tell she was shooting mad!

6 Dudes Find Loot

I unexpectedly had Saturday free. Mamaw was supposed to arrive on Saturday night, so Mom had warned us that we would be spending the day making our rooms "half-way decent". (She had set aside 9 hours for this, which seemed fair.) However, on Friday, Mamaw had called to say that she was postponing her trip because she didn't want to miss her Bible study.

It turns out Mamaw doesn't actually like traveling. I was surprised because my other grandparent--Dad's dad--loved traveling so much he bought an RV to do it in.

"She only *thinks* she doesn't like traveling," Mom said. "She'll enjoy herself once she's here."

"She'd have to actually get on the plane to do that," Dad pointed out.

"Why didn't she get on the plane?" Jayden asked.

"She likes things to be a certain way," Mom explained.

"She's fussy," Dad translated.

"She doesn't like the dry air on the plane," Mom explained.

"She should take a train," I suggested.

But Mom shook her head. "That would add too many days to the trip," said Mom. "She likes to be home in time to water her plants."

"Fussy," Dad said again.

While they were arguing, I went out to find the Dudes. They were in Ryan and Connor's yard. Nate was filming while Ryan demonstrated hand-based command signals.

"I got them from the U.S. Army Rangers handbook online," Ryan said. "They'll be useful whenever we're in earshot of the enemy or on any kind of covert action."

When we had practiced the signals a few times, we all got our bikes and headed over to No Man's Land for mounted patrol.

No Man's Land is what we call a patch of woods where nothing was built between Sherwood Lane and Sherwood Heights Drive. It's sort of the neutral zone between Sherwood High School and Sherwood Retirement Village. (I figure, if they ever had a battle, the high schoolers could totally take the old guys. For now, though, the two groups share an uneasy peace.)

No Man's Land is dense with trees and kind of hilly. And, like every patch of undeveloped ground in Sherwood, it's crisscrossed with dirt trails and frequented by walkers and bikers and dogs and wild animals too, like deer and coyote.

On the way over, we heard a deep rumble behind us.

"Car!" yelled Connor, but it was actually a package truck. Ryan signaled: "CONVOY HALT", and the Dudes got over to the side of Sherwood Lane to let it pass.

Nate elbowed me. "I recognize that driver," he said.

I looked in time to see the delivery guy who had interacted with Nate's Verbal Security System a couple weeks ago. He wasn't driving erratically, and his hands didn't appear to be shaking, so I guess no damage was done.

When the truck had passed, Ryan signaled: "MOVE OUT", and we proceeded to No Man's Land. Mr. Maguire told us that before they built the schools and the retirement village and the golf course, this whole hill was an untouched forest, and the trails were probably made by Bigfoot.

I knew from Grandad's work at the Sherwood Historical Society, that there had been Sammamish people in Sherwood before they were pushed out by European Americans. But they had *lived* in the valley by the river, not on the hill. Nate thinks it's most likely the trails in No Man's Land were made by teens seeking a shortcut to the high school.

The Dudes were here to do some mountain biking. It's more challenging than riding on the streets. And, after watching *ET* and *Stranger Things*, Ryan felt we should bump up our skills in case we're ever being chased by government agents.

Ryan signaled: "FILE FORMATION", and we entered the forest near the back fence of the Retirement village, following a trail that led around the boles of big trees and over small hillocks on its way to the top of the hill. When we reached the highest elevation, we had a choice of three trails to ride back down to street level.

Ryan signaled: "RIGHT TURN" and "HURRY UP", and Connor took the lead down the steepest trail. We all followed: first Ryan and Deven, then me and Nate. I stood on my pedals to cushion as I bumped over roots and rocks in the trail while leaving a bit of distance between me and the guys ahead. I didn't have any problem keeping up, but I didn't like to take the downhills at full speed either.

The path dipped down through a gully, draining my momentum. So, I had to push it to make the top of the next rise. Breathing hard, I plunged down the next drop, already leaning to make the sharp curve that I knew was coming up.

Unfortunately, Connor had had plenty of momentum through the gully. He'd popped at the top of the rise, hit the downside loose, and then wiped out on the curve below.

Ryan and Deven, who were close behind him, couldn't stop!

As I reached the curve, I saw Ryan try to signal "HALT" as his bike stuttered around Connor's. But it wasn't a good time to have one hand off the handlebars. His front wheel hit a root and jackknifed. Ryan bailed just in time to avoid ramming a tree.

Deven, coming fast behind them, was afraid to try to brake at that speed. So, he avoided the curve entirely, shooting straight off the trail and disappearing into the undergrowth.

Seeing the carnage, I slowed and ditched my bike, then went to help Connor out from under his own vehicle. As he eased himself to a standing position and tested his limbs, I saw Ryan crawling out of the bushes.

Meanwhile, Nate, bringing up the rear, rolled cautiously down the curve and parked his bike properly with the kickstand. Of course, the Dude with the most safety equipment hadn't been in the wreck. He took the mouthguard out of his mouth to ask, "What happened?" and then, "Where's Deven?"

"I'm okay!" called Deven's voice from the depths of the ferns. "These boxes broke my fall."

Boxes?

The rest of us pushed our way past the sprawl of salal plants and found Deven in a clearing. It was about as big as my bedroom and surrounded on all sides by high bushes and ferns. But the space in the center was clear of growing things (if you didn't count Deven). It would have been bare dirt, except it was covered in a layer of cardboard boxes and plastic bubble wrap and trash and, now, Deven's bike.

"Wow. I never knew this was here," I said.

"You think it's the site of a secret Native American village?" asked Connor.

"More like a secret village for slobs," said Deven.

"We're close to the high school," Ryan pointed out. "Maybe this is where teenagers come to hang out and drink beer and smoke."

"Do teenagers even do that anymore?" Nate asked.

"My sister doesn't have time," said Deven. "She and her friends hang out on their phones on the way to Math Tournaments."

Then I thought of something. "You think someone's been living here--like Sam did?" (Sam was this homeless guy we found two summers ago living in a fall-out shelter on the other side of Sherwood Heights Park.)

"If you lived in the woods, you wouldn't need window cleaner," Nate pointed out, holding up a full bottle he'd found.

"Or cat litter," Deven said, looking around. "Or...romance novels in Spanish?"

"Look at all the packaging around," said Ryan. "This is stuff people ordered online."

"Then why is it here?" Connor asked. "Did the package guy dump it?"

Nate and I turned to each other. "Porch Pirates!" we said in unison.

"Huh?" said Deven.

"Your mom was right," I told Nate. Then we explained how his mom had bought a doorbell camera to thwart package thieves and how Nate had enhanced it with Judge Grimm's voice.

"And that's why Dad's expensive fish food is at home instead of here in the pirates' den," guessed Nate.

"But if thieves took all this stuff, why leave it in the woods?" Connor asked.

"Because they didn't want to clean the windows after all?" Deven guessed.

"Think about it," Ryan said. "If you're a thief you steal stuff. But you don't want the stuff you steal. You want *money* to buy stuff you want."

"Probably to buy drugs," Connor put in.

"Probably," Ryan agreed.

"It's like back in 5th grade when we wanted Coconut Bucks to win the auction for the Elephant Gun," Nate realized.

"Except *we* didn't steal," I said.

"When you steal packages you don't know what you're getting," said Ryan. "It might be fancy jewelry or electronics that you can sell..."

"But it might be cat litter," put in Connor.

"The pirates must have brought the packages here to open them," I decided. "Then they took the good stuff and left the rest."

"So, they're also litterbugs," Deven pointed out.

"And look at all the cardboard they're wasting," said Nate. "That could have been recycled into something useful like more boxes..."

"Or funny hats," said Deven.

"Or armor for a tank," said Ryan.

But Connor pointed out the action item: "You know what, Dudes?" he said. "We've *seen* something. Now we've got to *say* something!"

Officer Racarro seemed a little nervous when we gathered around him at school the next morning.

"We've seen something," said Ryan.

"Yeah, so we've got to say something," said Connor.

The young officer gulped. "Really?" he asked. "Like a manifesto?"

"More like a mess," corrected Deven.

"Huh?"

"We think it's porch pirates!" said Nate.

"Arggh!" put in Deven.

Then we explained about the thieves' den in No Man's Land.

"We thought you could be Resource-ful and catch the bad guys," Ryan said.

"I know all about the package thieves," Racarro said. "Well, not *all* about them," he allowed. "But we've been getting theft reports for weeks."

"At Sherwood Middle School?" I asked.

"No, I mean the Sherwood Police," he explained. (Oh yeah. I guess he still works for them too.)

After school, we led Racarro and his partner, Officer Morgan, to the hideout in the woods.

"Cat litter, window cleaner, instant grits...," Morgan ticked them off in his notebook. "Yep, some of this is stuff that was reported stolen along with more expensive items that I don't see here."

"We think they sold those to buy drugs," Connor chipped in.

"Like Coconut Bucks!" added Deven.

"You were right to report this, boys," said Officer Morgan.

Then he clapped a hand on Racarro's shoulder. "That Resource Officer position is already paying off," he said. "We might just win the Community Policing Award from the county this year."

"What's the Community Policing Award?" Nate asked.

"It's an award that would show the Sherwood Police are in line with community values and don't need our funding cut," Morgan explained.

"Why would anyone cut your funding?" Ryan asked.

"Haven't you kids heard about people protesting the police around the country?" asked the cop.

Nate and I nodded. My whole family had gone to the city to attend the Black Lives Matter Silent March. And Nate's Mom was the one who had told us about it.

But Ryan shook his head. (And Connor and Deven were playing Slaps instead of listening right now.)

"Oh,..." started Racarro.

"Never mind," said Morgan, cutting him off. "We aim to show there are no bad apples in Sherwood!" he proclaimed.

"Um, okay," I said, not sure how apples came into it.

"Can we come with you when you arrest the perps?" Ryan asked, returning to the subject of the porch pirates.

But Officer Morgan shook his head. "We're a long way from an arrest, boys. We still have no suspects."

"Yeah," said Racarro. "It's not like we caught them in the act."

"Oh yeah," said Ryan, disappointed. Then his eyes narrowed. "Don't worry, he told the police. The Dudes are on the case."

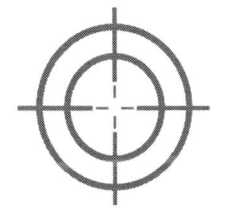

7 Dudes Empowered

We all thought the school was as hard as a target could get--that is, *after* they re-encoded all our cardkeys. But the PTA Security Council was determined to do something about Sherwood Middle's soft underbelly--that is, the students.

Mrs. Howe had brought in an expert to explain to the PTA how security classes would help students feel safer. I don't know what he said, but by the time the meeting was over, the parents were just panicky enough to approve funds for the classes.

Mr. Isaak didn't like the idea of empowering us--especially after he learned the empowering would happen in homeroom. He had a sour look on his face as he introduced our certified ASRaP instructor.

"What's ass wrap?" asked Deven.

"That's ASRaP," said the instructor. "**A**ctive **S**hooter **R**esponse **A**ssessment and **P**rotocol."

He had the fattest neck I'd ever seen. His head was shaved on the sides with a short brush of black on the top like the tip of a magic marker. And his eyebrows looked like they'd been drawn on with the same fat magic marker.

He told us we could call him Sargent Security or Sarge for short. (I figured, not telling us his real name was probably a security measure.) He was a big guy with bulging arms that strained the hems of his short sleeves. And he wore athletic pants with boots instead of tennis shoes.

"Better for hand-to-hand," Ryan whispered.

"Mom says he's ex-Special Forces," Nate added.

"Uh-oh," I said. "Doesn't she know all the bad guys in the movies are ex-Special Forces?"

"Really?" asked Connor.

"Sure," I answered. "How do you think they learn the skills they need to threaten major mayhem?"

"Ooh. Major Mayhem sounds way cooler than Sargent Security," said Deven.

"And ranks higher," Ryan pointed out.

Meanwhile, Sarge had been telling us that he wouldn't be using a lot of military terms or frightening images (like he'd done with the PTA, apparently).

"Schools aren't looking for that anymore, so I had to change my strategy," he explained. "My game plan is to meet you where you're at so you can wrap your head around what I'm telling you and see the method to my madness. By the finish line," he concluded, "we'll all be in the same ballpark."

"I will be in the teacher's lounge," said Mr. Isaak, quickly heading toward the door with mug in hand.

"Negatory! You should stay for this, Sir," Sarge cajoled. "You don't want your head in the sand on Judgement Day."

Mr. Isaak sighed. "I suppose not," he said, though his tone suggested he would also need stronger coffee on Judgement Day.

"Okay, Boots," Sarge said, looking at us, not his boots. (I found out later from my grandad--who watches the Patriotic Glory channel--that "boots" is what you call new recruits when they enter boot camp--which is not as fun as the word "camp" makes it sound. It's where they learn stuff like how to be a soldier and what all the jargon means.)

Sarge rubbed his meaty hands together. "We've got a lot to cover to get you action-ready. Of course, we want security to be fun. So, we're gonna play it like a game," he told the class. Then he lowered his eyebrows and added in a grim tone: "A game of survival."

"Cool," said Ryan.

But Nate raised his hand. "The odds of being killed in a school shooting are 1 in 614 million," he said.

"Don't worry, son. We're going to *do something* about those numbers!" Sarge answered encouragingly.

Sarge leaned forward with his fists on Deven's desk. Deven's eyes widened comically as the desktop flexed downward like a diving board.

"You guys are in seventh grade, right?" asked Sarge.

Deven nodded silently, but Teresa spoke up.

"We *girls* are seventh-graders too," she pointed out.

"Luckily, you guys are old enough to learn how to deploy an active defense," Sarge said. "And, when I say guys, I mean girls too, of course," he added, glancing at Teresa, who rolled her eyes.

"Guys of all races, creeds, and genders," Sarge added. "Like I told the PTA, security can be totally inclusive because it's all in our heads."

Nate raised his hand, "Do you mean the training program is VR?"

"Awesome!" said Connor. The Dudes were up for an Ender's Game-type scenario. (That's another great book, by the way!)

Unfortunately, Sarge shook his head. "We don't need fancy equipment. I'm going to teach you to make use of what's already here in the classroom," he said proudly. "And it works, believe me. I know because I *used to* wear football pads and let classes aim projectiles at my head." He smiled like he was remembering good times.

"In soccer, they tell us never to head the ball because it does serious brain damage," said Teresa.

Melanie nodded.

Connor spoke up. "My mom says getting a lot of concussions could make me angry and stupid later in life."

"How could you tell?" asked Ryan.

Sargent Security dropped the smile from his face and said, "My technique is more refined now. We're going to formulate action plans--just like the locker room before a game. That way, when the heat is on and the play is called, we'll know what we have to do to get safe home."

"You mean like, on the bus?" Connor asked hopefully.

"It's only homeroom," Teresa reminded us.

Sarge shook his head, which was no easy feat on that muscular neck. "I meant home like in baseball--you know, the goal, the score? It's a metaphor!" he announced proudly.

Then he clapped his hands. "Okay, so let's start by imagining that there is a guy with a gun who's entered the school. What question should we ask ourselves?"

"Do we have 24 hours to subdue him?" asked Ryan.

"Can he do moves like Jackie Chan?" asked Connor, knocking over a desk as he demonstrated.

"Will the president trade a high value hostage for our release?" asked Nate.

"Is it a guy-guy or a girl-guy?" asked Teresa dryly.

Sarge just grinned and crossed his bulging arms. Then he rounded on Mr. Isaak. "What would *your* question be, Coach?"

Mr. Isaak looked like there were a lot of questions he'd like to ask. He scratched his beard irritably and asked, "Can I get out of here?"

"Good one!" Sarge shouted, causing Mr. Isaak to twitch. "Up high!" Sarge said, holding his hand in the air over Mr. Isaak's head.

Mr. Isaak left him hanging. (I guess the power of high fives doesn't work on teachers.)

Sarge turned to the class. "The first question is always 'Can we get away?'" he explained. "You have a class evacuation plan and safe meeting place. Right?"

That was true. In the event of an evacuation, we were supposed to meet at the Starbucks two blocks away. I was pretty sure that Mr. Isaak had chosen that meeting place and maybe already had a standing order for a triple-shot grande. Of course, any shooter who properly cased the school would know that was the first place the teachers would head in an emergency.

"The question we *should* be asking is who let him in the door?" Teresa insisted. "We have all these security measures for a reason, and the students are the weak link."

"This *guy* makes a good point," Sarge said, clinging doggedly to his belief that guys can be girls. "It's important to think of the security measures not as inconveniences but as weapons in your arsenal."

"Awesome," said Ryan. "Can you teach us how to kill somebody with our cardkeys?"

Sarge's grin revealed teeth that looked like they could chew bullets. "You have the right idea. I'm going to teach you how to see your schoolroom as a fortification and ordinary schoolroom supplies as weapons and ammunition with which you can defend it."

This sounded like the kind of thing that Jayden was getting in trouble for doing at *his* school, but okay.

"Did you know you can use a rolled up magazine as a nightstick?" Sarge asked.

"That's sounds kind of old-school," said Nate. "Can we use an ereader?"

"I know how to use scissors like a throwing star!" volunteered Connor.

Sarge gave him a high five. But, about that time, the bell rang to end homeroom.

"I'll be back next week to teach you more," called Sarge, while Mr. Isaak began collecting all the scissors to lock in his desk drawer.

Over the next six weeks, Sarge bounced around to all the homerooms. And he taught us a lot. He said schools all over the country were teaching these techniques. Which, I guess, tells you something about the state of mind of parents all over the country.

"How many bad guys have they foiled?" Ryan wanted to know.

"Actually, nobody's used my techniques in a non-simulated shooter situation yet," said Sarge regretfully. "You could be the first!" he promised.

Nate pointed out: "It's actually more likely that the school will be struck by lightning or closed for a global pandemic."

But nobody thought that stuff was going to happen. We were preparing to fight off some guy with a manifesto.

"Is that like a balaclava?" Connor asked. (It's not.)

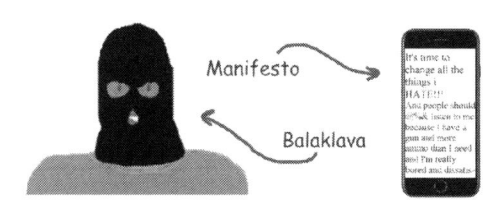

We learned engineering techniques to barricade the door. How to throw a stapler without damaging your rotator cuff. And how to swarm the assailant in a group to throw off his aim.

It was good that Sarge gave a lot of visual demonstrations because we didn't always understand what he was saying.

"Okay, guys. Everybody get in the huddle," he said one morning.

When we were ready, he gave us an imaginary defense scenario: "A shooter got past the outer defenses and we're in the hot zone. Do we try to go end around or do we blitz him?" Sarge asked.

When nobody answered, he hinted: "We don't want him to get us in the grasp, right? We want him to muff it--to end up with a pooch kick."

"What? No we don't!" argued Teresa who has a soft spot for pooches.

"Of course," Sarge went on, "if it were really happening now, when I'm here, I'd take him out with a chop block. You kids might give him the razzle-dazzle, but the point is to make him fumble," he explained in his distinctive way.

Then he added, "When the heat is on, and I'm not here, Mr. Isaak, will have to call an audible. So, okay, quarterback, what's our play?" he asked, tilting his head to pin his eyes on the teacher.

Mr. Isaak looked relieved to have been asked. "My back is aching," he said. "Can we discuss this from our desks?"

"Break!" Sarge ordered with a clap of his massive hands, and we all got back in our seats to discuss what would happen if the attacker got in the red zone.

"We've got two possibilities," Sarge suggested. "We could engage with smashmouth and hope to give him a slobberknocker, or maybe we draw him deep in a trap play and then employ a sneak. Get it?"

I looked around to see if anyone else had a clue. Blank faces stared back at me.

"Come on, guys!" said Sarge impatiently. "Most gamedays Mr. Isaak here is the quarterback. But on any given Sunday it could be up to the rest of you to win it in the trenches! That's why you've always got to have your game face on."

"I don't even know what game we're talking about!" complained Teresa. "And we don't go to school on Sundays."

She had a point. It was pretty confusing for kids who actually played or watched sports. Kids who weren't into sports had been lost for a while.

Ryan figured those of us who had a handle on battle tactics ought to help the others.

Luckily, Deven had recorded the whole thing. He started working on a translation right away. Maybe those SAT words his mom made him study would be useful after all.

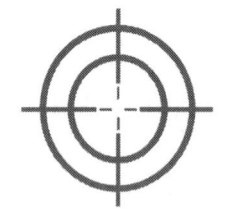

8 Dudes Decoded

Nate's mom was on a quest to threat-proof Sherwood schools. Through her research, Mrs. Howe had discovered that most mass shooters are former or current students. So, next, the PTA paid for teacher training on Student Behavioral Threat Assessment.

I figured Mr. Isaak was an expert on that already. But Nate's mom arranged for the teachers to take part in an online seminar on their workday.

Luckily, the teacher's workday is our day off! The Dudes spent it hanging out at my house. With Dad out in the shed (he didn't really have days off), the living room was pretty pleasant, despite the presence of my little brother, Jayden, who was also off school.

Turns out his class had intruder training too. But, while seventh graders were learning how to swarm and throw projectiles, the second grade had a different way of preparing for "any given Sunday".

According to Nate's mom, the elementary school has lots of security problems to overcome. For one thing, they go out for recess three times a day, and they are too little to keep track of cardkeys. So, you can't keep the doors locked all the time.

Plus, they are not hardened soldiers like us middle schoolers. Instead of learning real battle tactics with Sargent Security, the elementary school got story time with a book about ants.

"Ants?" I asked Jayden.

"Ants in *school*, obviously," Jayden explained.

(Right, 'cause otherwise it would be weird.)

"Wouldn't a pill bug be tougher?" Nate pointed out. "I mean, they have their own armor."

"Yeah, they're like a little tank," said Connor.

"We totally need a tank," put in Ryan, still dreaming of defeating Teresa.

pill bug with a rocket launcher

But I wanted to know more about this ant shooter scenario.

"Ants don't shoot. They're the good guys," Jayden informed me.

"Okay, then who's the bad guy?" Deven asked.

"The big bad wolf, obviously," said Jayden.

"Why doesn't he pick on animals his own size?" complained Deven. "Like pigs!"

I ignored Deven (usually the best policy). "So, how do the ants defeat a wolf?" I asked.

"They scatter and run serpentine," said Jayden. "That means like a snake."

"Okay. Run like an animal that doesn't have legs," I said. "That's good. What else?"

Jayden rolled his eyes back in his head, trying to remember. "I think the ants mostly Look and Listen," he said.

"Doesn't sound very intimidating," Ryan pointed out. "Especially to a wolf."

"Ants can be scary," said Connor. "Dad and I watched a movie where the ants were angry and wanted to take over the world," he told us. "They started with a sugar factory. Also, they were as big as a bus!"

"I like ants," said Jayden. "I think they're cute.".

Of course, he didn't stop with admiring them from afar. But we didn't find that out until later.

⊕

The only bad thing about homeroom with Sarge was that we now had homeroom homework. He told us all to go home and come back with a plan for how we'll react when (I'm sure he meant *if*) an active shooter gets into Mr. Isaak's room.

I stared at my blank shooter-plan worksheet and couldn't think of a thing. I know, I'm a writer, but I usually write about what already happen*ed*. I don't make up stuff I'm *gonna* do. Plus, it felt unnatural to come to school with any kind of plan. Usually, I just show up and let the day happen to me.

I was surprised to see Ryan's sheet was empty too, though. He's a plan guy for sure. Sarge's head wrinkled under his buzz cut when he saw it. But Ryan had an explanation.

"I didn't want to risk the plan being intercepted by the enemy," he said with a confident grin. "I've got it all in my head." He tapped his temple and nodded.

"Now you're thinking like a combatant!" said Sarge. Then he gave me and Ryan each high fives, which I took to mean I wasn't going to fail homeroom after all. Sarge is big on high fives. I guess he and Leon would get along.

Nate and Connor had both realized that the first and most important thing is to come up with an acronym to make your plan easy to remember. Nate's was a little long:

Surprise, **O**verwhelm, **M**ake **N**oise, **O**bfuscate, **L**ose, **E**vacuate, **N**ail, and **T**aze.

"S.O.M.N.O.L.E.N.T.?" I said, while Ryan was still scratching his head over it.

"It's not very action-oriented, I admit," said Nate. "But at least it spells something."

"Mine too!" said Connor: "**F**lummox, **Y**ell, **T**arget, and **S**warm!"

"You're going to have fits?" asked Teresa.

"Fights!" corrected Connor, who wasn't one to let spelling get in the way of a good acronym.

Deven figured this assignment was like homework from any teacher. All he had to do was fill the sheet with whatever they had said in class, and he would be golden. Only you couldn't just record what the teacher said with your phone and then use speech-to-text. (He'd found that out the hard way.)

"You have to restate it in your own words, man," he told me before class. He had recorded Sarge's metaphors and then translated them using words from his dad's golf and cricket videos.

Of course, Deven was happy to stand at the front of the room and read out his plan to the class:

When the big day comes, the most important thing is not to get the yips! Now we want the enemy to hit a cabbage, or at least a barkie. This is not the time for a chicken stick, right? We want to get him with a platypus.

Deven favored the class with a sparkling grin. Then he went on:

Now Ryan will pitch googly, of course. So, if we're lucky, the git will duck hook or hit a hosel rocket. Meanwhile, Nate keeps up the heat with a worm burner. It's no time for a dibbly-dobbly, so I'll aim a beamer. Then he'll get the same from Tyler at silly mid-off, Connor in the cow corner, and Teresa in the gully. As soon as we've given the tosser a sticky wicket, we'll slog sweep right past him and out the door!

Deven gave a deep bow while the rest of the class just stared.

"That made *no* sense," complained Teresa.

"Hey, no need for sledging!" Deven replied.

I don't know if Sarge ever played golf or cricket, but the terms seemed to translate. He gave Deven a high five as the bell rang and we headed out of homeroom to the less strategic part of the day.

In P.E., Coach Gregor let us out the doors so we could stand around the soccer field in huddled clumps. Usually Coach Rachel would be leading us in calisthenics as a prelude to running us ragged in a cutthroat game of flag football. Today, she didn't bother with the warm up.

She had forgotten the basket of vests and flags too, but she didn't send one of the students back for it. Instead, she suggested we take some laps around the field while she "watched our form" from the bleachers.

"Coach Rachel seems to have lost some of her enthusiasm for the job," Nate remarked as we passed the first turn and our "run" slowed to a bouncy walk. If you swung your arms, it looked enough like jogging to count. We called it "wogging".

"Yeah," I agreed. "It's like she's been taking lessons from Mr. Isaak."

"She's gaining weight too," Connor pointed out. He continued to wog but turned around to wog backwards so he could chat with us.

"I bet that happens to all P.E. teachers," Ryan reasoned. "Making kids exercise doesn't really keep the flab off," he explained. "It's more of a mind game."

"Ooh! Maybe she's going to become a female version of Coach Gregor!" Deven suggested.

I shuddered.

"Speaking of scary ideas," said Nate, "Mom found a Secret Service report that showed a connection between violent shooters and people who had been ostracized."

"Ostrich-cize!" said Deven, going into what looked like his chicken dance but with more head-bobbing and high kicks.

Coach Rachel had her head down and didn't seem to notice as we stopped to watch Deven and then just stood around talking.

Nate explained, "Ostracism is when people get left out of the group or bullied."

"Next, I guess we'll have to do an anti-bullying class in homeroom too," I said.

But Nate shook his head. "No, Mom says you have to catch kids young. The problem starts in elementary school, so it's already too late for us, I guess."

Coach Rachel roused herself to call from the bleachers: "Deven, are you injured?"

"No, ma'am," Deven called back, stilling his neck until she stopped looking at us. I saw her take an ice pack out of the first aid kit, but, instead of bringing it to Deven, she held it to her own forehead. (Definitely a Mr. Isaak move.)

"Anyway," said Nate. "Now that Mom's moved on to the younger kids, we're safe enough."

"Are we?" Ryan asked, his eyes narrowing. "What happens if the shooter comes when we're not in homeroom?"

I looked around. "Well, if he came right now, I guess we could run to the Starbucks," I said. "Come to think of it, that's a good reason not to use up all our energy on laps."

"Agreed," said Ryan, but he had a familiar gleam in his eye. "The problem is, we have a different class every hour," he pointed out, "and evil doesn't keep appointments."

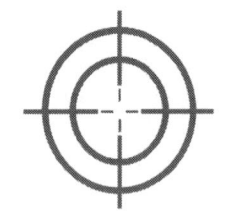

9 Dudes Arctic Assault

In November we got an early snow. Unfortunately, it came on the weekend, which meant three things happened:

1) We didn't miss any school.

2) Mamaw decided to postpone her trip until after the holidays because, even though she trusted the pilot, she said she was afraid that Dad would have an accident driving in the snow to pick her up from the airport and leave us all orphans. (So, I guess that was a good call.)

And 3) Well, maybe I'd better explain about the other thing that happened:

See, Ryan had one of his great ideas for what to do in the snow. In the past, we had used snow to build a mountain for sledding and skiing. And, of course, we had built a snow fort for battles. This year, Ryan's plan was to build enemies.

Every kid knows how fun it is to have a battle of some kind. But the problem can be finding someone to battle against. Battling girls or little brothers can get you in trouble. And, other than Ryan and Connor, the Dudes didn't really want to split up and battle each other. Besides, we don't have even numbers.

Ryan and Connor live right behind Sherwood Elementary School. And, when Ryan woke up that Saturday, a pristine field of snow beckoned to him from the playground. Gazing into the winter wonderland, he had a vision of white-clad ninja assassins. So, he grabbed some carrots from the fridge and called us over to start building our opponents.

Once we had a line of snowmen on the soccer field, we decorated them with eyes and noses and scimitars and stuff. (Ryan and Connor have the whole line of Foam Dart Company Chaos Melee weapons.)

When every frozen attacker had a face (and a weapon), we got Ryan and Connor's dart guns and practiced shooting the features back *off* of them. But it was actually pretty tough. Foam darts are light, so, even if you hit a bullseye, the bullet tended to bounce right off the eye rather than destroying it. Noses were better because sometimes they flew off the face--which would be totally funny in real life (or gross, depending on how you look at it).

"It's too bad Nani doesn't grow her tomatoes in winter," said Deven. "A really ripe one would make great blood spray."

Ryan promised to remember that for summer.

"We either need harder ammo or a more powerful gun," suggested Nate.

"I know a gun that is guaranteed to shoot out an eye!" said Ryan. He ran home to get the Elephant Gun.

(We had worked pretty hard a couple years ago to get our hands on an FDC Elephant Gun--a very rare but powerful dart gun. And shooting out an eye was the very reason they had been discontinued, and thus were so rare, in the first place!)

While Ryan was gone, my little brother, Jayden showed up at the school.

"What are you doing out of the yard, Jayden?" I asked. I lived in fear of a time when Mom would decide Jayden was old enough to follow me and my friends wherever we went.

"Mom said Rob and I could walk over to the school to see what you were doing," he explained. (I knew I shouldn't have told her where I was going.)

"Where's Rob?" Nate asked, looking around for the big shaggy dog.

Jayden shrugged. "He's coming." (Our dog was not the fastest walker.)

Jayden pulled a carrot off a snowman's face and started crunching it. "What are you doing?" he asked.

"Hey! You're eating our target," Deven complained.

"We're using the snowmen as enemy combatants and practicing our sniper fire," Nate explained.

"Cool," said Jayden, putting the half-eaten nose back on the enemy just as Ryan arrived with the Elephant Gun.

"Watch this, little Dude," he called, and squeezed off a round from about twenty feet away. It hit the snowman with enough force to send ice shards into the air and the carrot flying.

"Whoa! Cool!" shouted the Dudes.

The next round was a little high, but it blew the snowman's knit cap off. The third snowman lost his head entirely in a spray of ice chips.

While I collected the jumbo-sized, purple, Elephant darts (we only had three), the other guys rebuilt the snowmen. We went again, rebuilding between rounds, until all of us--even Jayden--had had a turn smashing heads.

About that time, Rob showed up. The big collie walked over to Jayden and sprawled in the snow.

"We can't go home now," I said. "Rob just got here, and he's too tired to walk back."

"No problem," said Ryan. "Modern weapons are too easy. Let's try some hand-to-hand."

By that time, our snowmen were in shambles, so we moved to another part of the field and built new ones. This time, we practiced defeating them with martial arts moves we had made up like "flying dragon kick" and "fist of death".

Next, we got sticks like the Mortal Blade on *Ninja Wars*. It took a quick and forceful slice to decapitate the snowmen with one stroke like Dawn Raider does to ninja demons on the show.

Then we tried fly-bys. That's where you run by, and, a minute later the snowman's head falls off. It's the kind of thing a ninja assassin would do (if he was in a hurry, I guess). However, it wasn't totally successful. It probably takes a sharper stick than we were using...or an opponent with an actual neck.

By the time we ran out of ideas for disfiguring snowmen, it was time for me to go home and feed Rob. He must have known it too, because he lurched to his feet. When he stood up, he took half the snow he'd been lying on with him.

His coat had grown out since we shaved an emoji on his flank in the summer. Now huge chunks of snow hung from him on one side.

"He looks like the Yeti's dog!" said Deven, taking a picture with his phone.

"The snow under him must have melted and then refrozen to his fur," said Nate.

"Come on, Jayden," I said. "We'd better go home and thaw our dog."

By Monday, the snow had melted off the roads, but there was still plenty in the yard. That didn't matter to the school superintendent, apparently.

"If the bus can get through, school's open," Mr. Guthrie told us when he picked us up that morning. (Actually, he had to repeat it to every kid at every stop.)

By afternoon, Ryan was working on a plan for a roadblock or maybe a pit trap. But the bus reached my stop before he thought of one, so I had to get off.

At home, I dumped my backpack, kicked off my shoes and flopped on the couch. I was enjoying the quiet of the living room in that hour before Jayden's school lets out when, suddenly, Dad tromped up the deck stairs and into the house from the shed.

I was surprised. Dad's shed/office has insulation and a space heater, but it's a cold walk across the slushy yard to the house. Dad hardly ever left his shed in winter before Jayden got home.

I quickly sat up and dove for the zipper on my backpack like I was just between homework assignments. But it turned out my work habits were the farthest thing from Dad's mind.

He held out his phone in a shaky hand as he announced, "I got a text from the school that Jayden was caught decapitating someone. That has to be a mis-type, right?"

He didn't wait for my answer but headed straight to his car to drive down to Sherwood Elementary.

Of course, Jayden was actually just *practicing decapitation* (which, come to think of it, wouldn't have sounded any better in the text). He and his friends had apparently used their recess time to build some more snowmen for mutilation purposes. But, for some reason, any form of decapitation makes the grown-ups at his school nervous.

The principal the Dudes had had at Sherwood Elementary, Ms Grieber, had retired after the Dudes graduated (just a coincidence, I'm sure). Jayden's school now had a new principal who seemed confused about the purpose of recess. There was already a rule that, on snowy days, students "may sculpt snow but may not pick it up." This was to prevent snowball fights, which, in my opinion, happen to be one of the healthiest ways to use fresh air.

Now, just because of Jayden, there was a new rule that students also "may not pick up or play with sticks", which meant all the sculpted snowmen would have to remain armless. (This is the kind of thing that happens when you try to mix two incompatible subjects like playing and school.) At least, because there hadn't been a rule when he did it, Jayden got off with a warning over the decapitation thing. He said he would stick to punching from now on, but he didn't get a chance to try out the new plan because we got a warm spell and all the snow melted.

It was nearly time for winter break. At the middle school, we were having a big clothing drive to help people who couldn't afford winter clothes. The early snow had kind of taken us by surprise, so, luckily, all my family's winter gear had already come out of the closets and was strewn across the floor of the mudroom for easy access.

Mom went through it, and I carried to school everything that she wasn't saving for Leon. It made me sad that there were people my size that couldn't afford to buy a coat.

I guess a lot of people felt that way because the winter clothing drive was a big success. Everybody brought stuff in bags which the school secretary had to keep in the hallway outside her office. Also in that hallway, was an equally big pile of warm jackets, winter coats, gloves, umbrellas and hats that were not in bags. They had been lost and found (but mostly lost) at school.

"Funny, I don't remember losing anything," said Connor as we perused the mound.

"Me neither," said Deven.

"I lost my gray hoodie," said Ryan. I could see at least fourteen gray hoodies in the pile. It would take forever to sort through them and find his.

"Nani always has extra gloves and hats when I can't find mine," said Deven with a shrug.

"I keep my hands in my pockets so I don't have to keep track of gloves," said Nate.

I wondered if there were any way Jayden's three missing jackets from last year could be in this pile.

"Mrs. Ritter, is this the pile from all the schools everywhere?" I asked.

She sighed and looked up from the work she was trying to do.

"Of course not," she said. "It's only things found here at Sherwood Middle. You boys better find what you're looking for. Anything that hasn't been picked up by winter break is going to be donated to the clothing drive."

"What happens to it then?"

"The nicer items will go directly to families that need them," she explained. "Anything else will go to Goodwill."

"That's cool," said Ryan, relaxing. "My hoodie will probably end up at the second-hand store where Mom can buy it again. She loves to save money that way."

At the last assembly before Winter Break, Mrs. Gutierrez gave a speech praising us for bringing in (or losing) so much winter clothing to give away.

"We can achieve so much when we work together as a community to help others," she said. "That's why, in the spring, I'll be assigning all 7th graders to do a Community Service project."

The Dudes didn't even bother to groan. Spring was all the way after winter break. That was too far away to worry about.

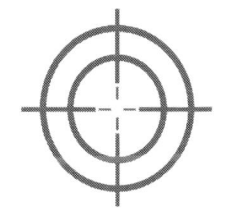

10 Dude Delinquent

Unfortunately, when Winter Break was over, Mrs. Gutierrez reminded us about our community service project. Ryan decided to get some expert advice.

"Hey Teresa," he asked. "Do you know what to do for the service project?"

"Of course," said Teresa, flipping her ponytail. "Melanie and I started planning the first day Mom announced it."

"What do you mean *planning?*" he asked. Ryan was the king of plans, but I guess he never thought of using his genius for school.

"Service projects are pretty much like writing papers," Teresa said. "You need a topic. Then you need three arguments for your three paragraphs. Then you need three pieces of evidence for your arguments. It's a structure, you know?"

The Dudes nodded, but I'm pretty sure Nate was the only one who had a clue what she was talking about. With papers, I usually just started typing what I was thinking and kept going until I had enough paragraphs.

"I looked on the internet for how to complete a successful service project," Teresa told us. (Whatever she's doing, Teresa always looks it up first to find out the best way of going about it. I think that's kind of cheat-y. But her mom's the principal, so, I guess she has less lee-way to screw up than a lot of kids.)

Oh yeah, Teresa was still explaining her brilliance:

"I just followed the rule of threes:

"1. I found a group that needs help--dogs.

"2. I found something that plays to my strengths--organizing.

"And, 3. I have a goal--to raise enough money for a dog water fountain to be installed at the off-leash park."

It figures Teresa would do something for dogs and forget about how thirsty the rest of us get. I took Rob to the off-leash park one time, and I got more exercise than he did.

"I have three sources of funds," Teresa went on, "businesses, people, and dogs. And I have three reasons we need the fountain and three reasons to donate and three ways to get people's attention."

But something she said had gotten *my* attention: "Dogs? You're going to get money from dogs?" I asked.

"Just wait and see," she said.

10 DUDE DELINQUENT

There was one good thing about this assignment, though. We could team up to do our good deed. And I already had a team. The Dudes decided to meet at my house after school to come up with a plan for Operation Dude Deed.

Of course, before we got much planning done, we were interrupted by Jayden skipping in the door and Dad plodding in behind him. Yes, Jayden was sent home early again--this time for wearing a hat.

"I don't remember you having a hat this morning," said Dad.

"I made it at school," said Jayden, showing us the hat. "It's like Freebooter from *Urban Space Pirates*. I could only make it with big paper like they have at school."

The Dudes reacted positively, and Deven tried on the hat.

"What's the problem with wearing a hat?" I asked. "We used to have 'Hat Day' when I went to Sherwood Elementary."

"It's a security risk," Nate explained. He'd been reading all his mom's school shooter safety materials. "It could obscure someone's face."

Jayden turned pale. "Is obscured like what happened to the man in the moon?" he asked. (Jayden is afraid of the man in the moon.)

"No!" said Dad quickly. "The man in the moon has nothing to do with school." Then he added, "But you'd better not wear a hat anymore, just to be safe."

"That's a pretty lame rule," complained Ryan, who frequently wore an Indiana Jones hat himself. "I mean, baseball players wear hats."

"And beekeepers," added Nate.

"And everybody in black and white movies," put in Connor.

"My dad's golf visor is only half a hat," said Deven.

"My mom wears a hat to church on Easter," said Nate. "I do find it suspicious, since she never wears a hat any other day."

"I'm sure the school has a good reason like...if everyone obeys the rule, it will be easier to tell who the intruder is?" said Dad uncertainly.

"So, in Jayden's case, they could have mistaken him for a four-foot intruder wearing a paper hat?" I asked.

"That would be a *good* disguise if you were trying to impersonate a second-grader," Connor pointed out.

"Nah, they're onto hats now," Ryan scoffed. "The intruder would do better to walk in with just an AR-15."

"The important thing is not to get in trouble so they don't call me to pick you up!" said Dad, glaring at Jayden. "You've missed the last hour of the day seven times this semester. What class it that anyway?"

"Sharing and Stretching," Jayden answered.

"Man, I miss elementary school!" said Deven with a groan.

"Hey. Maybe our service project can be about helping the little Dudes," Ryan suggested.

"I don't know. They've got the moms on their side," I said, "...and, uh, dads," I added, trying to be polite since Dad was still in earshot.

"Yeah," said Connor, "and they've got this school shooter thing covered, what with the hat ban and all."

"Wait," I remembered. "Didn't Nate say they wanted an anti-bullying class?"

"That would be a great subject for our service project!" said Ryan.

"Can we teach that?" I asked.

"Sure!" said Ryan confidently. "We just have to learn it first."

"We already taught Jayden and his friends how to be Dudes," Deven pointed out, referring to Jayden's 6th birthday party, which had been Dude-themed.

"It's true," said Nate. "We're influencers. That puts us way ahead of teachers when it comes to being listened to."

"But we don't know anything about bullying," I pointed out.

"That's because peer pressure is so much more effective," put in Ryan.

And Connor added, "Plus, no one is ever mean to us besides Teresa."

"If we don't know anything about bullying, how are we supposed to teach second graders?" I asked. Actually, I wasn't even sure if we were supposed to teach kids not to bully or not to *be* bullied.

Ryan scoffed. "You think teachers know math before they start teaching it?"

"So who's going to teach us about anti-bullying?" Connor asked.

"Dad knows what it is," I said, remembering our discussion a few weeks ago. But, when I looked around, I realized Dad had slipped out and gone back to the shed.

"Easy," Ryan declared. "All we have to do is get our parents to spill what they know. Then we turn around and teach it to the elementary kids."

About that time, Mom came home and shooed the Dudes out. She had been pretty tense all week, but now she exuded this calm efficiency, like a Battle Ninja preparing to fight the Infinity Beast. It seems Mamaw had finally run out of excuses not to fly across country, so she would be here tonight.

Mom had brought take-out, but we didn't get to watch TV while we ate. Instead, we had to sit around the kitchen table while she drilled us on a bunch of manners we don't usually use, but which she said Mamaw would expect.

Mom promised heavy punishments for all the stuff we're used to doing too, like leaning on our elbows or drumming our silverware on the table (even if it's a real song). We weren't supposed to mention if we didn't like the food. And, even if we liked it, we weren't allowed to smack our lips.

After dinner, Mom sent Dad to pick up Mamaw from the airport. Meanwhile, Mom ran around the house picking up clutter with one hand and vacuuming with the other.

She grabbed all her exercise balls and rubber bands and weights out of the dining room and piled them in my arms and told me to dump them in the basement. It reminded me of times I've helped Dad get ready for Mom to come home. I guess everybody's mom is scary.

"Mamaw will be tired when she gets here, so we need to get her room ready," Mom said. Then she sent me up to my room to take the Battle Ninja sheets off the bed and put on the plain white ones she bought just for Mamaw's visit. Which didn't make any sense because the Battle Ninja sheets go with the decor better.

"Why do *I* have to give up my room for Mamaw?" I complained even though we'd talked about it every night this week.

Mom sighed and said, "Because your room is closest to the hall bathroom. And, by the way," she warned. "You and Jayden and Leon should use the master bathroom for the duration."

Did you know that "for the duration" is a phrase people used to use in wartime? I guess that tells you what state of mind Mom was in about Mamaw's visit.

"Go right now and move Leon's stool and potty chair so Mamaw won't trip over them," Mom commanded.

I didn't want to touch Leon's potty chair. It was a toilet, after all, even if he just sits on it with his clothes on. Still, I could tell Mom was in that mood where more talking would remind her of more chores, so I decided it was best to get out of her sight.

I went upstairs and told Jayden to move Leon's potty chair to Mom and Dad's bathroom. I carried the stool Leon uses to play with water in the sink when he's supposed to wash his hands.

Last night after dinner, when Mom told us the sleeping arrangements, I had asked very reasonably, "Where am *I* supposed to sleep? Can I go live with Nate again?"

"No!" Mom had explained as she pawed through the clean laundry. (She had decided to do all the laundry and choose our clothes "for the duration" too. I guess she didn't think Mamaw would be a fan of the stuffed-in-a-sack look Dad created with his Smart Laundry Plan.)

"Mamaw is coming all the way across country to see you," Mom had said.

"And me!" Jayden put in. He was excited about Mamaw's visit because she always brought presents.

"Yes, and Jayden and Leon," Mom had agreed, frowning as she picked up the third toddler shirt in a row that had stains. The stained ones she tossed in a pile on the floor. So far, there were more clothes in the pile than folded in the basket.

"You can sleep with either one of your brothers," Mom had told me.

I chose Jayden's room because it was closest. Luckily, I hadn't unrolled my sleeping bag yet from my visit with Nate. I just chucked it across the hall and I was set. I had forgotten that Rob also sleeps in Jayden's room. More on that later.

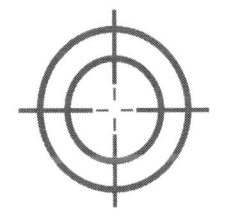

11 Dudes At Home

Mamaw was a small woman. She looked shorter and grayer than her picture on the mantle. Which is funny because she said we kids were the ones who had changed since she last saw us.

When Mamaw arrived she was tired, just like Mom said. She didn't even comment on the clean floors or the faintness of dog-smell. She pulled gifts out of a tote-bag she was carrying. Then she kissed the top of each of our heads (everybody but Rob). As soon as that was done, she went up to her (my!) room to bed.

"Mamaw crossed three time zones to get here," Dad explained. "Where she lives, it's already late."

"I hope she won't have jet-lag while she's here," Mom worried.

I figured Mamaw would sleep well enough in my bed. But things weren't so easy for me in Jayden's room. First, I had to listen to all the things Jayden was planning to show Mamaw when he got home from school tomorrow.

Second, I had to listen to him tell all the same things to Rob when he came in.

Yep, I had forgotten that Rob sleeps in Jayden's room. He flopped down on the floor next to my sleeping bag and panted in my face like my own personal doggy furnace. I solved that problem by flipping my sleeping bag so that Rob would pant on my feet instead of my face. Of course, his tail slapped me upside the head a few times, but that stopped once he conked out, which was fast. Eventually, Jayden stopped talking and I fell asleep too.

Sometime in the night, though, I dreamed that the school shooter was chasing me and my legs were paralyzed. I woke up to discover that Rob had moved over onto my sleeping bag during the night. He probably liked the slippery nylon because it felt cool.

Anyway, I was trapped. Rob doesn't follow orders, so I couldn't command him to stand up or roll over even if I wanted to make noise and wake up the Twilight Chatterbox. In the morning, I had to squeeze myself out of the sleeping bag like toothpaste out of a tube.

Mamaw was up way early.

"I'm chipper as a bird," she told me when I slogged into the kitchen. "By my watch, it's already ten o'clock," she said, turning her wrist so I could see. Mamaw told me that keeping her watch on home time prevented jet-lag. I guess it worked because there she was making pancakes on a weekday, filling lunchboxes, and volunteering to babysit Leon while Dad and Mom went to work.

At school, the Dudes and I tried to come up with a three-point system like Teresa:

1. Who needs help? Little kids.
2. What are we good at? Influencing little kids.
3. What is our goal? To teach little kids about bullying.

"I would change that to "teach kids how to *prevent* bullying," Teresa suggested when we showed her our idea. "And how are you going to *do* that, anyway?"

It was just like Teresa to tell us all we needed was three points and then expect us to have a whole plan. Luckily, Ryan was good with plans.

"Don't worry, Teresa," he said. "We're going to go to the elementary school and we're going to teach the kids about bullying, and then we're going to *influence* them not to do it!"

"Good luck with that," said Teresa, like we were proposing something a lot more complicated than a water fountain for dogs.

We didn't have to convince Teresa, but for our plan to work, we did have to convince Jayden's teacher. After school, I went to Deven's and started writing an email with phrases like: "raise awareness", "counteract aggressive impulses", and "promote unity".

I got them from Mrs. Gutierrez's speech at the See Something/Say Something assembly. It's all security, right? Deven had the audio file. His plan of recording the adults in his life instead of wasting time listening was paying off.

When I got home that night, it was already time for dinner in Mamaw's time zone. Luckily, Dad had made chili in the crock pot and Mom came home early from work.

While Jayden and I were gone to school, Mamaw had taught Leon a new trick. She sat on the couch and asked to see his toys. Leon would run off to get a toy and bring it and wave it in Mamaw's face.

"Wonderful!" she would say. Or "I like that one," or "Isn't that neat!" just like she'd never seen a toy truck before. She would give him a high five. (Of course! Apparently, they do that back East too.) Then she would cleverly and enthusiastically say, "What else?" And Leon would run back to his room to get another toy. Judging by the pile of toys in the living room, they had been doing this all day.

At dinner, Mamaw said, "I had forgotten how much work the little ones are." Then she added, "I don't know how you keep it up and your job too, Meg."

I thought that would please Mom, but, instead, she frowned. "*Jason* is at home, Mom," she said.

"Well, yes, I suppose..." said Mamaw, like she thought Dad would just hide in his office all day and never interact with the kids...which, to be fair, was probably what he had done all day while Mamaw was looking after Leon.

"And Jason's dad takes Leon to Stroll'n'Step, on Mondays," Mom added, "and to Beethoven Babies twice a week and to Bilingual Story Time at the library and to Little Swimmers on Fridays."

"Goodness!" said Mamaw. "In my day, we just let them play."

"I'm pointing out that Leon isn't missing anything while I'm at work," Mom said.

"I thought that's what *I* was saying," said Mamaw.

Meanwhile, Leon, sensing that Mom and Mamaw were paying more attention to each other than to him, decided to wave his spoon to get attention. A kidney bean flew off and hit Dad (who was eating with his head down).

As Dad wiped his hair with a napkin, the dinner table fell silent (a common side effect of the no lip-smacking or silverware-drumming rules).

"Well," said Mamaw in an obvious bid to change the subject, "what did you big boys do at school today?"

"Me! Me!" said Jayden, raising his hand. I guess the uncomfortable silence had made it seem like school.

"What did you learn today, Jayden?" asked Mamaw with an expectant smile.

I saw Mom tense and Dad looked up with a spoonful of chili halfway to his mouth.

"I learned about science," said Jayden.

The fear on Mom's face melted into a smile as Jayden continued.

"Did you know that bees do a lot of the work of growing food?" he said. "It's not plowing. It's pollination!" he announced.

"Why yes," said Mamaw chortling at his joke. "That must be why we say 'Busy as a bee!'" she said, winking at

Jayden and deftly catching Leon's bowl as he pushed it off his tray.

"And what did you do at school today, Tyler?" she asked, turning to me.

Finally, an opening. "Um, we talked about bullying," I said. (Well, we did until Ms Fletcher told us to be quiet and pay attention to the math lesson.) "We're supposed to talk about it at home too," I pointed out. "Mrs. Gutierrez sent an email."

"She did?" Mom asked.

Just then Dad's phone dinged in his hand where he was hiding it under the table.

"Uh, yeah," he said, looking up sheepishly. "She just did."

I grinned and crossed my arms. Teresa came through. I knew she would convince her mom after Ryan had *implied* that Einstein Academy had a Family Discussions Initiative to talk about sensitive issues like bullying. Teresa had ranted that public school was every bit as good as private school, and that her Mom would prove it.

Now Mrs. Gutierrez was making our parents chat with us about bullying. All I had to do was absorb the information. I grabbed a pencil and the pad of sticky-notes by the phone.

"I just want to remember this," I said.

Mom looked at Dad and smiled. Then Dad frowned after Mom made him hand over his phone.

"We're supposed to discuss three questions," Mom said, wiping a smudge off Dad's screen with her napkin. Then she read aloud: "1. What is bullying?"

"It has to do with milk!" said Jayden, forgetting to raise his hand.

"Miwk," agreed Leon, whacking his milk off his tray.

While Dad chased the sippy cup across the kitchen, Mamaw looked at Jayden in confusion.

"He means someone taking your milk-money," I translated, earning a smile from Mamaw.

"Oh, yes," said Mamaw. The fact that she recognized the milk-money thing reassured me that Dad wasn't completely off his rocker after all.

"That's *one* kind of bullying," I hinted. (Teresa had said that every question has three answers, so I was looking for two more.)

"A bully might take things or threaten people," Mamaw said.

"He could karate chop them," suggested Jayden. "Or call them a dweeb or have a secret club and not let them join."

"Those are all good answers," said Mom nervously. It probably looked like Jayden was in training to *be* a bully. "Tyler, do *you* have any ideas?" she asked, shifting her focus to me.

Uh-oh! I had been thinking of this activity as a listening exercise, not a reporting one.

"Um," I began hesitantly, "like if you really like quattro cheese chips and somebody else says quattro cheese tastes like goat turds and they act all high and mighty like nobody should hang out with someone who doesn't like "flavor blasted" best and then maybe they get you in a headlock," I concluded.

"That was...very specific," said Dad.

(That's because it was a real incident. It didn't happen to me, but to two other people I know, who shall remain nameless.)

"Basically, bullying is making someone feel bad or not being nice to them," said Mom, winding things up and moving on to the next question.

I wrote down "not being nice". I would work up a better way to say it later.

"Question 2. Why should we be nice to other people?" Mom read.

"That's assuming we're *not* the bully," said Dad with a chuckle. But Mom glared at him.

This was a hard one. I mean, I'm pretty much nice to people. But I never thought about there being a reason. Maybe I was born nice, which raised the question: Could you be born a bully? And, if so, did the rest of us have to be nice to you about it?

"Um, maybe so people won't think you're a bully?" I guessed.

Mom bit her lip and turned to Jayden, hoping for another "helpful bee" answer, I guess. "What do you think, Jayden?" Mom asked. "Why are you nice to someone?"

"'Cause maybe they have a dart gun I like to borrow," explained Jayden practically.

Then Mamaw put her two cents in: "What about because God tells us to love each other?"

I was pretty sure that wasn't it. But Mamaw was confident. "Jesus asked us to care for one another," she said.

I wrote down "religious beliefs", but I knew I couldn't use it. For one thing, Jesus was definitely one of those people who was born a nice guy. For another thing, we couldn't use him for Operation Ruffian Rout (Bully Bulwark? Thug Foil?) because we couldn't talk about religion at school. If I wanted answers I could use, I needed to redirect the conversation.

I started by writing down "Jesus" in big letters. It couldn't hurt to show Mamaw I knew how to spell His name. Then I said, "He's not the only one, right? I mean, doesn't every religion tell you to be nice?"

Mamaw frowned. "Yes, I suppose..."

"And, if that's true," I went on, thinking of Nate, "isn't it possible that aliens are pushing religion to make us soft and easy to take advantage of?"

"Don't call people aliens, dear," said Mom with a nervous smile.

"I mean space aliens," I explained. "That is, Nate means space aliens," I corrected, in the interest of clarity.

"We were talking about God, not space aliens," said Mamaw stubbornly.

I didn't want to quibble with Mamaw, but God is a non-human who lives in the sky, so, technically...

"I see now why Mrs. Gutierrez wanted us to have this conversation at home instead of school," said Dad with a chuckle that fell flat.

I could see what he meant. Religion and space aliens were just two of the topics we weren't allowed to discuss at school. There were also: sex, how to cheat, and video games. It's one of the protections under the law so that everybody gets the same education by leaving all that stuff out.

"I'm all for separation of church and state," said Mamaw, frowning at Mom, "but, if my grandchildren are not being churched at home..."

I had never heard anyone use the word church as a verb--not even at Nate's house, and they went to church every Sunday. Our family was more the type that almost go to church on Easter and Christmas but we can't remember what time it starts so we sleep in instead.

"What's the Church state?" asked Jayden. He had a puzzle of all the states, and he knew Church wasn't one of them...at least I hoped he did.

"That's 'the separation of church *and* state,'" said Dad. "It means we don't talk about religion at school..."

"So no one will feel left out or *bullied*!" put in mom triumphantly.

"Right!" I said, relieved that we were back on track. "If Mr. Isaak had a grudge against Christians, he would bully Nate. But, since Mr. Isaak has a grudge against kids, he doesn't pick on anyone in particular."

And that answered question 1, I realized. Bullying is picking on some*one* instead of everybody and making them feel, uh, not-part-of-everybody. I scrambled to fit all this on the sticky-note.

"Uh, maybe we should move on to the third question, Meg," Dad suggested.

She gratefully looked down at his phone.

"3. What should you do if someone is being a bully?" she read. "Mom?" she said graciously to Mamaw. "Why don't *you* tell the kids what they should do."

"Yeah, Mamaw. What would you do back in your day?" I asked, figuring to get a cool story like out of Little House on the Prairie.

Mamaw got this misty look in her eyes like she was looking back through the eons. Then she told her story:

"There was a tough boy at my school. He liked to tease the younger children to make them cry. He wasn't in my grade, but we all waited in the schoolyard before school, and he would pick on us--pull our hair or swipe our books. One time he took my book report poster that I had worked so hard on. When the bell rang, he let it fall on the ground, and it got a smudge. I was so angry!"

"Did you call Jesus?" Jayden asked. (Yeah, he was probably picturing a light-up Jesus Signal shining across the sky.)

Mamaw hesitated. "Well, I'm sure I prayed about it," she said, "which is the right thing to do. But I also told my brother, Dan," she admitted. "He was quite a bit older than me and already out of school. He started driving me to school and hanging around the schoolyard before work."

(That blew my mental picture of covered wagons out of the water.)

"Even on the days he couldn't come, I told everyone he was 'around somewhere'", Mamaw admitted with a grin. "With someone big and tough standing there watching, that bully wouldn't try anything. And I was safe the rest of the year."

"Just like Batman!" said Jayden.

Okay, so it sounds like Mamaw (and Jayden) were advocating solving one bully with another. Finally, an answer I could use!

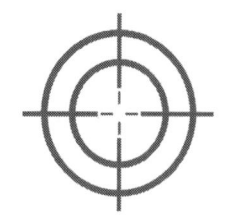

12 Dude Influencers

That night, I moved my sleeping bag to Leon's room. Leon had already been asleep in his crib for a couple hours. I figured I could look forward to a quiet, dog-breath-free night.

It must have been nearly dawn when I was awakened by an odd humming sound. I could see the barest hint of light around the edges of the blackout shade that mom had put on the window to keep Leon from getting up too early.

It wasn't working. The sound I was hearing was definitely Leon, humming a song from Beethoven Babies. I held my breath, hoping he would fall back asleep.

Instead, he stood up and climbed over the side of his crib, stepping on my stomach before he reached the floor.

"Tywer!" he screeched happily, like I had just come home from school.

"Hey, buddy," I responded groggily. "I'm sleeping now, okay?"

"O-kay!" Leon chirped. I guess he expected a high five, because he leaned over and patted my belly. Then he waddled over to his toy bin.

Great, I thought. Maybe he'll play quietly so I can get back to sleep.

But, a few seconds later, he was back by my side, waving a stuffed-monkey in my face.

"No, Leon," I said. "I don't want to see your toys right now. I need to sleep."

Leon dropped the monkey on my face and toddled away. But in a second, he was back with a truck. I was glad I had left the monkey on my face when he dropped that too. It bounced off the monkey onto my chest. I grabbed it and said, "Gentle, Leon."

"Gentle Weon," agreed Leon, laying the next toy gently on my stomach.

By the time Mom came in to wake me for school, she almost couldn't find me. Wearily, I crawled out from under the mound of vehicles, animals, and puzzles and staggered into the empty hall bathroom. A glimpse of Mamaw's lotions on the counter reminded me that my stuff was now in Mom and Dad's bathroom. So, I turned around and shuffled back to the other end of the hall.

While I brushed my teeth, Mom did her make-up and Dad looked over my shoulder in the mirror to shave. Leon came in to watch us, sitting on his little potty seat with his pants on.

Suddenly, Jayden pushed to the front of the crowd and turned on the sink full blast.

I stepped back to give him space, bumping Dad, who nearly took off a sideburn.

"Jayden, what are you doing?" Dad asked, annoyed.

I pulled the toothbrush out of my mouth.

"He's rinsing his hands, Dad," I said, sidestepping just in time as Jayden turned off the water and shook his hands wildly. Drops splashed the mirror, the counter, and Dad's shirt.

"He does it every morning," I explained from behind Dad.

"My hands get hot from sleeping," added Jayden.

Dad looked like he wanted to say something, but Mom spoke first. "This is exactly why I didn't want the boys sharing a bathroom with Mamaw," she said. She gave Leon his high five and then tripped over his potty chair as she left the room.

I went to school optimistic that the other Dudes had gotten more useful info than I did for our bullying presentation (I mean *anti*-bullying presentation). Not that I was complaining about Mamaw's solution to *her* bullying problem, but I wasn't sure it was scalable. I mean, if every kid had a tough big brother...well, the bullying problem would probably be at home rather than school. Plus, *I* was Jayden's big brother. I didn't want to be on the hook for protecting him.

On the bus, we separated out the useful knowledge (like actionable items) from the stupid stuff (like Dad jokes).

We had plenty of answers about what bullying was. But, surprisingly, none of the parents had been much help on what to do about bullying once you recognized it. Deven's mom, who was a lawyer, had advised Deven to write a detailed email complaint. She said the important thing was to keep a paper trail of all communications with the school.

Deven's dad had said the key was to immerse yourself in your studies so that you had grades that would take you to university a year early, as he did. Then you could become a doctor early, retire early, and have more years to play golf.

Mrs. Maguire had laughed at the idea that her boys were in danger of bullying from anyone but each other.

And Mr. Howe had said "I would consult your mother, of course," which Nate immediately did. That's when Nate's mom had gotten this look on her face that Nate calls "The Teaching Moment Twinkle".

"Great! So, she taught you what to do?" Ryan asked.

Nate sighed. "No. She doesn't like to provide answers if she can encourage research instead."

Mrs. Howe had given Nate a whole accordion folder full of links for useful webpages and pamphlets with counseling techniques for talking about sensitive subjects with young children (some of which she had tried with Nate when he was Jayden's age).

We had time to look through it all in homeroom. Ever since we finished defense training with Sarge, Mr. Isaak used homeroom time for staring down at his desk and rubbing his head.

"What's this?" asked Deven, grabbing the most colorful thing he saw.

"It's a Talking Stick," said Nate.

Actually, it was a dowel rod about 18 inches long that had been painted yellow and had a bell and some colored feathers glued on the end.

"It's a tool to facilitate discussion," Nate explained. "Only the person who is holding it can talk, and everyone else has to listen."

"Ooh! This must be the stick Teddy Roosevelt said to carry when you speak softly," said Ryan, snatching it from Deven and brandishing it at his brother like a saber.

"I always imagined it bigger," said Connor, ducking.

"What's the Circle of Empathy?" I asked, pulling out a chart that looked like a Venn diagram from math.

"It doesn't matter," said Ryan confidently. "All we have to do is make a video of us teaching it to Jayden's class."

"First they have to let us *in* to Jayden's class," I pointed out. "I never got a response from Ms Finch about our offer to teach."

"Better write her again," Ryan urged.

This time, when I emailed Jayden's teacher, I decided it would make us look more professional to follow Deven's mom's advice. So, I mentioned a lawyer had advised us to keep a paper trail. (Then, to be safe, I printed out all the emails so they would be on actual paper.)

This time, to my surprise, Ms Finch responded right away that she would be happy for us to take up an hour of class time. I guess professionalism pays off.

Jayden was excited that afternoon when I told him the Dudes were coming to his classroom.

"You can see my desk, Tyler," he offered. "I've been organizing it."

"Yes, he has," said Mamaw with an almost-concealed shudder. She had gone to pick up Jayden from school today so she could see his classroom and meet his teacher. (While she was gone, I knew Mom had sneaked in her room to see that she hadn't started packing yet. We were all wondering if she would really get on the plane tomorrow.)

Anyway, Mamaw doesn't wear a hat, so, no one at Jayden's school had mistaken her for a criminal or anything. And, speaking of criminals, remember that ant book that the second grade read to be prepared for a school shooter? Well, Jayden and his friends had gotten really interested in ants after that. They started watching them on the playground during recess and discovered that they do, sometimes, run serpentine.

I was impressed. Between the dust of the soccer field and the cement of the tetherball court, there isn't much healthy vegetation on school grounds, so it was surprising that they found something alive on which to focus.

At first, Jayden and his friends had watched the ants during recess. Then they got the bright idea of taking the ants inside where they could watch them better. Of course, ants won't just sit around in your desk while you do your spelling.

Mamaw led us into the kitchen, where we found Dad leaning against the counter, reading his phone. He put the phone down when he saw Mamaw.

"I think you should buy some more of those little lunch containers," Mamaw announced.

For three days, Mamaw had been packing our lunches with fresh fruit and homemade sandwiches instead of the pre-packaged stuff Dad usually gives us. She even cut the crusts off. But the important thing is that all this stuff went in little plastic containers--round ones for the fruit and square ones for the sandwiches. We were supposed to bring them home to be washed and re-used.

Dad was leaning toward his phone, trying to keep an eye on his notifications. "What?" he said, looking up. "No, we've got plenty," he said. He walked toward the sink and opened an empty cabinet. Then he started checking all the cabinets.

"We always had enough before," insisted Dad. "Tyler, you unload the dishwasher. Are you doing something with the little containers?" he asked.

"What would I do with them?" I asked evasively. (Actually, since Mamaw seemed to enjoy taking part in the local chores, I had let her unload the dishwasher this week. But it didn't seem right to pin the missing containers on her.)

"You could keep ants in them," suggested Jayden while Dad kept looking.

"What for?" I asked him.

"For pets," he said. "They're interesting."

I didn't agree. I mean, you can't teach ants to bring you a ball or anything (although our dog, Rob, won't bring you a ball either). Anyway, ants only work for themselves.

While Dad searched the kitchen, I told Mamaw and Jayden about this ant farm Nate had once. Apparently, the ants had thought of it as more of a prison camp, because they staged a breakout and infested Nate's Dad's secret stash of chocolate. (That was back when Mrs. Howe was making him avoid sugar instead of gluten.)

"Ants can farm?" Jayden wanted to know. "Like bees?"

I shrugged. "Nate said they just needed to be properly motivated," I replied.

"Wait," said Dad, breaking in to our conversation. "Jayden, what do you mean about keeping ants. Do you know where your missing lunch containers are?"

"They're in my desk, Dad," Jayden confessed. "Miss Finch said I should work on desk organization, so I've been using the containers to keep my ants organized. I take them out at recess for play time," he added. "But I always put them back."

Maybe it wasn't such a mystery why Jayden's teacher wanted someone *else* to run the class for an hour.

Mamaw had been listening politely to my story, but now she announced cheerily, "Yes, we found the missing lunch containers! Jayden will bring them home after school tomorrow when he releases his...pets," she said with a grimace. "But you should probably buy new ones for food anyway," she suggested.

She smiled at Jayden and kissed him on the head. Then she kissed me on the head. Then she announced that she was going to go start packing for her flight home tomorrow morning.

"Gotta get on that plane!" she said.

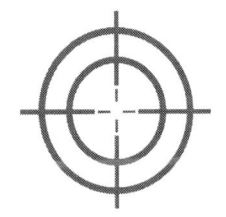

13 Circle Of Dudes

The only cool thing about this service project was that it gave us an excuse to miss a morning of school. Sweet! Of course, we had to spend that morning in Jayden's school. But at least the Sherwood Elementary teachers couldn't assign us homework anymore.

After being Connor's 5th grade teacher, Ms. Finch had switched to teaching second grade, which is why Jayden had her. She actually seemed glad to see us, which tells you something about her positive attitude, I guess.

"I have such fond memories of your class's 5th Grade field trip to the state capitol," she said.

Ryan grinned. "You mean when Connor got lost and Nate's robot was mistaken for a bomb and Deven's grandmother nearly started a revolution?"

"What?" said Mr. Howe, his gecko eyes darting between Ms. Finch and Ryan.

Oh yeah. The school had insisted that we have an adult chaperone despite the fact that we were supposed to be the teachers for this hour. Luckily, Nate's mom had volunteered her husband for the job.

"Time to get started!" Nate declared, quickly ending the conversation. He set up his tripod to film the action.

As usual, the Dudes were totally organized. My job was communication. Ryan and Connor had made up scenarios for role-playing, Nate would do the filming and editing the video so we could get credit for the project, and Deven was in charge of the talking stick (he had already put googly eyes on it).

First, we pushed the desks back and made the kids sit down in a circle on the rug.

"This is the Circle of Infamy," Deven announced.

"Empathy," I corrected. I could see I would have to be on my toes to make sure we communicated the right message.

"Right," said Deven, "so we've got to make it as big as possible."

"And we all hold hands to show we care about each other--even the girls," Connor warned. The little kids had no trouble with that. I guess they are more evolved than middle school kids.

A little girl raised her hand. "What's empathy?" she asked.

"It's like sympathy," said Ryan knowledgably, "only without the S. You can look it up later," he suggested.

"Or watch our cosplay demonstration!" Connor put in.

"Role-play," I corrected. We had decided we didn't need costumes because of how we already looked like kids.

Ryan, Connor, and Nate went to the middle of the circle for the first role-playing scenario. Connor pretended to trip, then fell down on the carpet and gripped his leg.

Nate and Ryan stared down at him.

"I fell down on the playground," Connor called to them.

"You goof! You're so clumsy," said Ryan, pointing at him and laughing.

But Nate knelt down and said, "Are you hurt? Let me help you."

The players stood up and took a bow to show the scene was over.

"Now, who was empathetic?" I asked.

Jayden's friend Cello raised his hand. "*Connor* was pathetic because he fell down," he said with certainty.

"Yeah, it *was* kinda pathetic," agreed Ryan.

"I could do it better!" Connor promised. "Let me go again."

"Not pathetic, *empathetic*!" I reminded everyone.

The kids just stared. I tried to do what Mamaw said and think of Jesus. I don't know if it was His idea, but I tried rephrasing the question.

"Who was nice?" I asked.

Right away, all the kids recognized that Nate was nice and Ryan was mean.

Ryan, Connor, and Nate took another bow. Then they tried to return to their places in the circle, but the second graders wouldn't release hands to let Ryan in.

"The mean guy shouldn't be in the circle," said one little girl.

Another one agreed. "We don't want mean people here," she said.

"Yeah, we're nice!" growled Cello threateningly.

I was beginning to be worried for Ryan's safety.

"Whoa!" I said, going for a teaching moment. "You wouldn't want to be Ryan and get left out of the circle because you were mean. Of course, no one should be left out of the circle," I added hastily, "even Ms. Finch and Mr. Howe," I said, because they were sitting on chairs while the rest of us sat on the floor.

"Maybe if we're nice to Ryan, he'll be nice too," I suggested, raising my eyebrows at Ryan.

"Uh, yeah," he jumped in. "I'll be nice from now on," he promised. But the little kids wouldn't let Ryan back into the circle until he showed he was nice by apologizing to Connor.

"I'm *sorry*!" he said grudgingly. "In fact, I'll show you how sorry I am when we get home," he added.

From there, we decided to move on to Deven's part.

"This is Gabby the Talking Stick," he explained. "He's here to vacillate discussion."

I wanted to correct him, but I wasn't holding the stick.

"You can only talk when you're holding Gabby," Deven explained. Then he turned to me for our rehearsed demonstration.

"Tyler, why did the chicken cross the road?" he asked me. But I zipped my lips closed and refused to answer.

Then Deven gave me the stick, and I opened up and said, "I don't know, Deven, why did the chicken cross the road?"

I handed the stick back to Deven, who used Gabby's high voice to say, "*Because he was stapled to the punk rocker! Ha, ha, ha, ha, ha!*"

Deven (and Gabby) laughed like crazy until the little kids pretended to get it and laughed too.

"Gabby has a great sense of humor!" said Deven.

Next, we passed the stick around the circle, trying to get the class to talk about times they had been bullied or had done the bullying. It's called "safe sharing". But they kept passing the stick back to Deven to hear Gabby's silly voice again.

Luckily, I had prepared some leading questions.

"What would you do if someone took your milk money?" I asked and was proud when Jayden's hand shot up. But, once he got the stick, he just wanted to explain to the other kids how they might be able to use their lunchroom cards for purchasing new skins in video games.

We sort of got off on a tangent there, and I saw Ms. Finch looking at the clock.

I hurriedly grabbed the stick back and asked a question before she could jump in and get control of her class.

"What should you do if you are bullied or see someone being bullied?" I asked.

The kids started passing the talking stick around the circle. As I watched Gabby pass from hand to hand, I worried that either Connor or Ryan would use it to bash each other on the head, but they passed it on until Jayden's friend, Alex, took it.

He spoke into Gabby's head like a microphone, saying, "I would tell the teacher."

I figured that was sort of passing the buck, but Alex was probably right. Besides, I didn't have a better answer. I mean, none of our sources had any information on what an adult was going to do about the problem. Would a teacher stand around guarding the kid like Mamaw's brother, Dan?

Curious, I asked, "And what would *you* do, Ms. Finch?"

The second-grade teacher took the stick thoughtfully. "First, I would make sure that the person who was being bullied was all right," she said seriously. "And...I would get them back their milk card, or whatever," she added uncertainly. Maybe she was too young to have ever carried milk money to school.

"Then I would talk to the person who had performed the bullying behavior," she continued, on surer ground. "I would tell him or her that he had made the other person feel bad and why that wasn't a nice thing to do." Then she finished strong: "And I would inform his or her parents so they could impose consequences."

"Great answer!" I cheered. I could tell she was trying really hard to make our project work. And it would look great on the video. Then I turned to the only parent in the room and asked, "And, as a parent, what would *you* do, Mr. Howe?"

Mr. Howe looked up suddenly when the talking stick came between him and his phone. He frowned into Gabby's googly eyes. His gecko eyes bulged. His gecko neck got red.

I wondered what, if anything, he had heard of the preceding discussion. I looked at Nate, but his eyes were focused down in his lap, and he was wiggling like he was uncomfortable. Probably embarrassed by his dad, I guessed.

I was pretty sure at this point that Mr. Howe wouldn't have the answer, but I took the stick from him so I could at least feed him the question again.

"Suppose Ms. Finch told you that Nate had been bullying someone," I said. "What would you do?" I handed him the stick again.

Mr. Howe seemed unsure why he had to hold the stick, but he took it. He glanced between Gabby in his left hand and the phone in his right hand. Then he took a second look at his phone. His eyes bulged a little more. Then he looked up at me and spoke.

"I would implode conservation?" he said, and handed the stick to me.

Nate made a strangled noise and wiggled again.

Mr. Howe snatched the stick back. "Oh! Impose consequences," he said with a nod. Then the bell rang for recess.

⊕

"Stupid autocorrect!" Nate complained when our Bullying Seminar was over and he didn't have to hide his phone in his lap anymore.

The little kids had gone to recess and Mr. Howe had gone back to work, and we were walking home from Jayden's school. Jayden's class was going to make anti-bullying posters to decorate the lunchroom after recess, but we could take credit for that without actually being there.

"Yeah," I agreed. "But it was lucky your dad looked at his phone in time to read your text," I pointed out.

"That was a given," said Nate. "Dad never misses a text in case it's from work."

Luckily, we could edit "implode conservation" out of the video.

"But what does 'impose consequences' even mean?" Connor asked.

Deven had an explanation. "It's what teachers say when they want to pass the buck to the parents. And it's what parents say when they haven't thought of what the punishment is going to be yet. If you're lucky, they never come up with anything!" He appeared to be speaking from experience.

Later that week, the Dudes got a nice card from Ms. Finch thanking us for visiting her class. We also got Jayden's anti-bullying poster. She said it was "so creative" that we would probably want to enjoy it at home instead of putting it up on the lunchroom wall with the others.

It showed the lunch lady taking away Jayden's pizza gun and demanding milk money from Alex while Cello snuck up behind her with the talking stick. He really captured the crazed expression in Gabby's googly eyes. (And in Cello's.)

I decided to let Dad handle the consequences on that one. The Dudes had done our job.

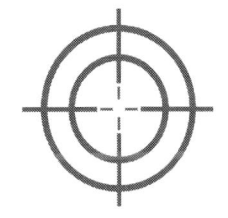

14 Re-Dudes, Reuse, Recycle

The Dudes' service project was a winner, of course. There would surely be fewer bullies in future generations. (I had my eye on that Cello kid.) But there were a lot of good service projects that spring.

And the Dudes weren't the only ones to make use of free labor from the parents. For instance, Shannon and Dalaja called their group The Green Team. Mrs. Gutierrez let them send an email blast to all the parents asking them to save the shipping boxes from one week's worth of online orders. Then their kids brought them to school, and The Green Team piled them on the tennis courts.

This created an impressive heap, which the Dudes admired from the bus on the way home.

"Why did you put all the boxes on the tennis courts?" I asked the girls, who were sitting in front of us.

Dalaja twisted around in her seat. "Because of the high fences, so they won't blow away," she explained.

"What are you going to do with them all?" Nate asked.

"Film them," Shannon answered.

"They're not doing much," Ryan noted. We passed the tennis courts as Mr. Guthrie turned out onto Sherwood Road. The boxes reached nearly to the height of the school bus.

"We're going to show the pile on the school website and on the Sherwood Heights Neighborhood website, and maybe TikTok," Dalaja explained.

"What for?" Connor asked.

Dalaja shrugged. "In case somebody wants to do something about it, I guess," she said.

"You mean impose consequences?" Deven suggested.

The girls looked at each other. "Sure," Shannon said.

The Dudes nodded sagely, which was what most of the adults were doing who were driving by too. It was a really big pile of cardboard. Somebody should do something about it.

Ryan was on top of that. "When you're done filming, I have an idea how you can get rid of it," he said.

When the Green Team was through with their display on Wednesday, the Dudes went over to the Maguire's house. Deven used his phone to show Mrs. Maguire the Green Team video. Then Ryan and Connor told her that we had to help with the project by moving the cardboard.

"All the way to the transfer station?" she asked.

Mrs. Maguire had just gotten off work at the hospital. I could tell because she still had a ridge in her hair from where she had taken the ponytail elastic out.

"Not that far!" said Connor quickly.

"To a suitable site in Sherwood," Ryan reassured her.

Mrs. Maguire bit her lip. "Well, it's right when I should be cooking dinner," she said, "but, if it's to save the planet, I guess I can do my part." Then she added, "It's lucky we have a crate of frozen pizzas from the Warehouse Store."

"That's not luck," Ryan argued. "That's just good planning."

Of course, "a suitable site in Sherwood" was my house. The Green Team had been lucky with dry weather for three days. Ryan figured, to *keep* the cardboard dry, we'd need a large, covered storage place--like my basement.

First, Mrs. Maguire drove us back to the school and parked beside the tennis courts. Then she laid her head back against the headrest of the driver's seat and turned on The Grateful Dead.

"Is your mom all right?" Nate asked, while the Dudes started flattening boxes.

"She looks like she would be grateful to be dead," I pointed out.

"That's how she always is after her shift at the hospital," Connor informed us.

"She won't ask any questions as long as we do the work," Ryan added, slicing tape with a wicked-looking box cutter.

It was a *lot* of work. Even with the back seat out and cardboard piled in our laps, it took three trips to empty the tennis courts. I guess the Green Team wasn't wrong about the amount of stuff people were ordering. And this didn't even count the boxes that were stolen by the porch pirates.

In my driveway, Mrs. Maguire listened to the Dead, gratefully, while the Dudes unloaded the boxes, carried them through the side yard and tossed them through the sliding door to the basement.

Dad didn't come out of his shed/office. And it wasn't the first time I was glad that the windows on the shed are too high to see out of.

I don't know what Mrs. Maguire thought my parents were going to do with all that cardboard, but she left feeling really good about how she'd helped the environment while getting in a nap after work.

"Mom likes to multitask," Connor said.

It'd probably be better for the planet if she drove a smaller car. But somebody has to drive a minivan. Otherwise, the Dudes would be dependent on Deven's sister, Shaila, and her SUV in situations like this.

On Monday, we had saved the elementary school from bullies. On Wednesday, we had helped out the Green Team with recycling cardboard. On Friday after school, Teresa--with Teacup in her arms--was waiting for us when we got off the bus in our neighborhood. Of course, she had a job for us.

The Social Media Club would be hosting what they called a Neighborhood Give and Take event at the school on Saturday. Apparently, their event was key to Teresa's service project too, and she wanted our help.

"We already did our project, why should we help you?" Ryan growled.

Teresa wisely dodged that question. "You'd be helping the *Social Media Club*," she pointed out. "They need workers."

For obvious reasons, the Social Media Club had had no trouble with advertising their event through all the internet channels. In fact, everyone was talking about the Give and Take *online*. But, somehow, when it came to actually showing up in person and doing stuff, they hadn't had many people willing to commit. (Maybe that should have been obvious too.)

"You should help because it's Service Week, and it would be a service to the Community," Teresa argued.

I was surprised when Ryan said, "Okay."

"Wait! What do you want us to do?" I asked warily.

"Bring your dog," Teresa told me, letting Teacup lick her cheek.

"Huh?"

"Dogs aren't usually allowed on school property," Teresa explained. "But, if you're working at the event, no one will mind if you bring him along."

I was confused. Teresa's usually all about following the rules, not breaking them. Plus: "Why would I bring my dog to the Give and Take?" I asked.

Teresa sighed, like it was a pain to have to let us boys in on her kooky plans. "I'm going to have a booth there," she explained. "I want Rob to help me collect donations for the dog water fountain."

"Rob can't count change," I joked.

Teresa rolled her eyes. "All he has to do is hang around looking thirsty," she told me. "Teacup will do all the *real* acting," she added, giving the Chihuahua a squeeze.

Acting? I figured Rob could handle the part. With all that long hair keeping him warm, he was pretty much thirsty all the time anyway.

Then Ryan said, "Don't worry, Teresa. We'll *all* be there bright and early."

Teacup growled, and Teresa gave Ryan a suspicious look--which was probably all the thanks we were going to get--before she turned and flounced off, ponytail swinging.

The Give and Take was supposed to be sort of like a garage sale. Only there was no money involved. Everyone was invited to bring stuff they wanted to get rid of, and everyone was invited to take whatever they wanted, first-come-first-served.

"This is a lucky break," Ryan said, rubbing his hands. "We'll get first choice on everything that's brought in."

I just hoped we wouldn't have to store it in my basement.

On Saturday morning, my breakfast was disturbed by the sound of Mom piling stuff in the mudroom. I slurped the rest of my cereal milk and went to check it out.

I saw Leon's outgrown pack-n-play and stacks of used-for-the-last-time baby clothes and a whole pile of those toys you get from buying a kids' meal.

"Tyler, there you are," said Mom like I'd been hiding from her or something (which, I was worried maybe I should have been).

"I'm collecting things to take to the Give and Take," she said. Apparently, getting rid of stuff was worth getting up early on her day off. "We're going to have a lot more room in this house!" she vowed. "I sent your father down to get all the old jigsaw puzzles from the basement closet."

Uh-oh.

I raced to the basement stairs in time to see Dad coming up with a dazed look on his face.

"Well, where are the puzzles?" Mom asked.

"I, uh, didn't find them," said Dad.

"I told you right where they were," said Mom. She had that WHY AM I THE ONLY ONE WHO KNOWS WHERE THINGS ARE voice. That's the voice she uses whenever I ask her something like "where's the ketchup" or when Jayden says he didn't do his homework because he didn't have paper.

"I guess I have to go down there myself," she complained, starting to push past me.

"No!" Dad and I said at the same time, which caused him to shoot me a suspicious look.

"There's nothing down there," said Dad in a panicky voice.

"What?" said Mom. "That's where we always kept the puzzles. Where could they go?"

"Um, they could be recycled!" I pointed out. "Jigsaw puzzles are cardboard, you know."

"Yes," said Dad, looking dizzy. "Lots of cardboard."

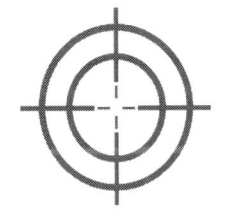

15 Dudes Give and Take

"I'll help you load this stuff in the car, Mom," I said, grabbing an armful of slobbered-on stuffed animals. Here's a little tip: nothing distracts parents like offering to do work without prompting. It's so surprising, that they immediately forget whatever it was they were going to ask you about. Of course, you can't go there too often or it loses its surprise (not to mention the danger that they'll start *expecting* you to help out).

I loaded the giveaway stuff in the car. Then I loaded Rob in the car. Then I had to go back to the kitchen to collect Mom, who was still puzzling over my unexpected helpfulness.

When we arrived, a lot of stuff had already been dropped off and more residents were arriving to peruse the selection. A few of the social media club members were standing around the snack table (looking at their phones, of course), but the Dudes were already getting things done.

Nate was arranging books into an approximation of a Minecraft-style Angkor Wat. Deven was playing with the baby toys. Connor was trying out sports equipment. (I didn't know if he was looking for new football pads or protection from Ryan.) And Ryan was directing traffic as parents arrived and unloaded their stuff into the parking spaces. This was his strategy to get first dibs on anything good.

Teresa's friends, Melanie and Anusha were arranging stacks of baby clothes into "cute" and "gross". I left Rob with Teacup at Teresa's booth and joined Ryan. He handed me a roll of tickets to give out to everyone who donated.

This is how it worked: You got a ticket for each item that you gave. And each item cost a ticket to take. That was a pretty good deal if you brought in baby socks and took home furniture. (Well, depending on the decrepitude of the furniture.)

"Keep an eye out for anything useful," Ryan told me as he directed a dad with an armful of computer cords.

Mrs. Gutierrez had explained that this wasn't like a marketplace, where the point was to make money. The point was to reuse all this stuff in the most efficient way possible, which meant it was a good thing if people got a good deal. The Taker was happy to get stuff for free, and the Giver was happy to make room in their house…for more stuff, I guess.

Mom had brought lots of baby stuff. But she only gave me a few of the tickets even though probably all of Leon's baby clothes had been mine originally.

"I don't want to take anything home," she had told me in the car. But now I saw her snag one of those no-pedal scooting bikes for Leon. She went to put it in the car, but she came back again, clutching her tickets.

There was a lot of junk I thought nobody would want like: used doorknobs and movies on VHS tape, and books about cat psychology. But pretty soon, it looked like everybody in Sherwood was there. And everybody found something to love.

Deven's sister, Shaila, took home a whole stack of teen fashion magazines from the eighties.

Deven's grandmother snagged some wireless speakers that look like rocks for her luxury outdoor room.

Mr. Maguire found a comfy leather chair for his apartment and a tarp for his girlfriend's truck (which he was using to bring home the chair).

Grandad found a foldable charcoal grill he could use when he was RV-ing. He also got a welcome mat that said "Happy Camper".

Nate's dad chose a bucket full of pump filters for his koi pond. They weren't the right size, but he said he could cut them down. And Nate found a floating alligator decoy that he hoped would scare the raccoons away from his dad's fish.

Connor got one of those mini-trampolines which I figured he would use to do stunts and Ryan figured he would use to injure himself.

I used some of my tickets on cans of green and gray spray paint. The guy who brought them had also brought a rusted metal patio table that he had failed at sprucing up, but the woman who took the table was planning to use different colors.

Deven found a rainbow parachute--the kind they use in preschool for the kids to lift up and down and crawl underneath. I knew from Grandad that they used them at Beethoven Babies too.

"Maybe Nate could rig it like a real parachute for jumping out of a plane," mused Ryan, which made me glad nobody brought in a plane.

Meanwhile, a bunch of people were saving tons of money that they would have normally spent buying and shipping new stuff instead of choosing to love something old because it was free. In fact, they apparently felt so good about the money saved, that they were happy to shower Teresa with it.

Her booth put on a show every fifteen minutes in which Rob walked slowly from one side of the booth to the other and then panted heavily. He did a very credible job of acting tired and thirsty. Then his friend, Teacup, pushed a little bowl over with his nose which Teresa filled with a splash of water. Rob obligingly lapped the water up with his giant tongue while Teresa explained how the dog park needed a water fountain.

When she was finished, Teacup would pick up the little bowl and walk around the crowd, collecting donations. It was a total success as long as you didn't mind fishing your earnings out of a slobbery dog bowl (which, apparently, Teresa didn't).

By afternoon, Mom had gone home (with a full car), and the Dudes had tried out all the furniture, putting our feet up on the tables and lounging in the chairs. Unfortunately, we didn't find anything that would fit in the dojo. We had just finished a battle using donated dart guns (almost none

15 DUDES GIVE AND TAKE

of which worked more than twice in a row) when a woman pulled into the parking lot in a pickup that said Hardware Home on the side.

"Am I too late?" she asked. "I had to rent a truck."

Ryan glanced at what she had in the pickup's bed. "Not at all, ma'am," he said in his best please-the-parents voice. "Just pull right around through the bus lane there, and we'll help you unload."

I was confused, because the bus lane was going to take her to the back of the school, but Ryan was giving his silent command signal to RALLY, so the Dudes left the Give and Take area and circled around back.

When we got there, Ryan had directed the woman to back into the space behind the dumpsters. Then he lowered the tailgate, climbed into the back of the truck, and directed the rest of us to help him. That's when we got a look at the woman's cargo.

"It's a geodesic dome," said Nate.

"Huh?" said Deven. "It looks like a climber."

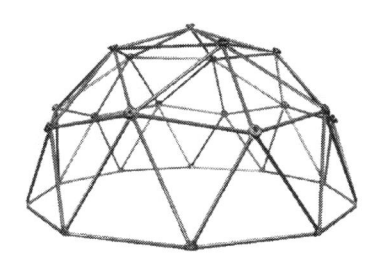

"My girls used it for years," said the woman. "But now they're too big for it and I want to put in an outdoor living room," she said, watching us lift it down to the ground.

"Oh, do you watch Luxury Outdoor Living?" Deven asked, distracting the woman from the fact that we were hiding the climber behind the dumpsters.

"Yes! Isn't it wonderful?" gushed the woman. "I probably can't afford much, but I want to put up a pergola and some drapes. Maybe I can find something here."

"I would suggest a screen for gaming and a putting green," said Deven.

The woman glanced around to see that the truck was empty. "I hope there will be someone here who can use the climber," she said.

"Don't worry, ma'am. It'll go to a good home," Ryan assured her. "Here," he said, handing her a fistful of tickets. "You can use these to buy anything you want at the *Auxiliary* Show Plaza around front," he said, directing her with a gesture back toward the Give and Take area.

"That was all our tickets," Connor complained when she was gone.

"We don't need them," said Ryan. "We got exactly what we wanted."

At the end of the Give and Take, a truck from Goodwill came to collect all the leftover stuff. (All except the "gross" pile of baby clothes, which the Green Team put in the Retex bin to have the fibers recycled.) When the Social Media Club finished filming each other sweeping the sidewalk in front of the school, the event was over.

Time for the Dudes to figure out where to take the climber and how to get it there.

"We can't leave it behind the dumpster. Mr. Swenson will throw it out," I said.

"It won't fit in Mom's minivan," Connor warned.

"We should have asked the lady to deliver it with her truck," Nate realized too late.

Ryan sauntered over and lifted one side a few inches off the grass. "This thing isn't that heavy," he said. "We can carry it."

"Carry it where?" Deven asked.

"To Tyler's house, where else?" said Ryan.

"We're not gonna put it in the treehouse are we?" I asked.

"The diameter is too big for one of the platforms," Nate pointed out.

"It doesn't go in a tree," Ryan declared. "This thing is mobile."

But, when we had spaced ourselves around the dome and picked it up, we found the limits of its mobility. It wasn't that heavy, but the bars bumped against your knees and, with all of us in a circle, it was hard for Ryan to lead. We basically managed to move it a little farther behind the dumpster before Ryan called a halt.

"It's too far to walk to my house, even if we *weren't* carrying a climber," I pointed out.

"Yeah. That's why we take the bus," said Connor.

"Sure wish we had Mr. Guthrie here right now," said Deven.

"He'll be here Monday morning, won't he?" said Ryan. "Maybe we can talk him into making a little delivery for us."

So, Monday morning, on the bus, the Dudes sat in the front seats instead of in the back. We had a lot of explaining to do before we got to the middle school.

"I don't mind dropping it off, boys," said the bus driver. "But it won't fit through the doors."

"That's why we brought supplies," said Nate, pulling the dojo rope out of his backpack like a magician doing a trick. "We can secure the cargo to the *roof* of the vehicle. I advise using a trucker's hitch."

"And don't worry about lifting it," said Ryan as we arrived at school. "Help is on the way."

There's a little set of aluminum stairs which Mr. Swenson climbs to fill the dumpster. As soon as the doors opened, Deven and I moved the stairs next to the bus. Meanwhile, Connor ran to the gym and brought back Coach Gregor. (Getting help in any situation is usually a matter of finding an adult who won't ask questions.)

"I appreciate your help," said Mr. Guthrie to the coach pleasantly. It was strange to see him outside the bus...and standing up.

Coach Gregor grunted unpleasantly. Then he squatted in front of the dome and wrapped his meaty hands around two of the angled junctions where the poles were screwed together. With another grunt, he jerked the climber up and over his head in a single motion. Then he pressed his legs straight up to standing and straightened his arms to vertical.

Hastily, Mr. Guthrie and I draped Ryan's fleece Seahawks blanket over the roof of the bus to prevent scratches. Coach Gregor climbed the steps with the dome in his hands and lowered it onto the fabric. Then he released his grip and stepped away with a nod.

"Perfect!" said Mr. Guthrie, and the Dudes clapped and hooted.

Coach Gregor's slash of a mouth twitched slightly, which might be as close to a smile as he could get. Then he turned and pounded back into the school building.

Nate helped Mr. Guthrie thread the ropes through the windows and tie the dome to the top of the bus like a Christmas tree. The rest of us ran toward the back door of the school. The bell was ringing, but I held the door open so Nate wouldn't have to find his cardkey.

Mr. Isaak didn't ask us why we were all late together that morning. He just sighed.

That afternoon, when we got to our bus stop in front of Teresa's house, there was the climber, waiting for us. There's a tracker on the bus, and Mr. Guthrie is only allowed to go to authorized stops.

"But there's nothing to say the bus can't be a little heavier than usual," he told us with a wink. Luckily, the same stop is used by the high school kids who were waiting when Mr. Guthrie arrived this morning.

"It took three football players and two wrestlers to help me get your dome off the roof before I drove them to school," he reported, handing Ryan his Seahawks blanket and Nate his rope.

"We owe you one, big time," Ryan told him as we got off the bus.

Fortunately, from there we only had to walk the dome around the corner to my yard. Unfortunately, right about that time, Teresa came riding by on her bike.

She says she likes to turn around in our cul-de-sac, but I think she does it to keep an eye on us. Why else would she even ride this direction when there are no thru streets? And why would she slow way down and ride beside us in the bike lane instead of passing on by?

She had Teacup in a little basket on the front of her bike. When he saw us, he started yapping.

"What's this?" Teresa asked over the yaps.

"It's a geographic dome!" said Deven.

"He means geodesic," Nate corrected with a gasp. He wasn't the only one who was already out of breath.

"I can see that," Teresa said. "Where did it come from?"

"From the Give and Take," Connor answered. "Ow!" he added as the dome banged his shin.

"My dog booth did very well at the Give and Take," Teresa informed us, stopping her bike as we arrived at my yard.

We stood there holding the climber as a show of strength.

"Teacup and I raised a lot of money," she said. She gathered the Chihuahua into her arms so he'd stop drowning out her bragging with his barking.

I wished Teresa would leave so we could set the dome down and take a break. But she snuggled her face against the dog's.

"He's a wonderful actor, aren't you, boy?" she cooed.

I felt sweat popping out on my forehead, and my arms were about to fall off.

"Rob did well too," Teresa added generously. "And I met a city councilmember who has a pug and who said she would help me get a permit for the fountain." She probably could go on all day, but Ryan broke in.

"Guess you better get on that before she forgets her promise," he warned. "You know how politicians are."

"Oh! You're right!" said Teresa. She dumped Teacup back into the basket and put her feet on the pedals.

The Dudes managed to wait until she had disappeared around the corner before we finally dropped the dome and collapsed in the grass.

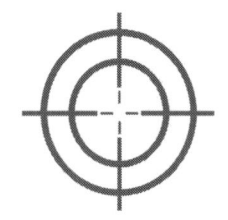

16 Dudes Lock Down

The next day in homeroom, we had homeroom-work *again*. This time we all had to write thank you notes to Sarge telling how much we had learned in Safer Homeroom.

"It's a good thing, too," Nate told me. "The PTA is giving a prize to the most prepared class at an assembly this afternoon. And there's going to be a scheduled lock down drill to test us today."

"In homeroom?" Ryan asked.

Nate shook his head. "I don't know. It's supposed to be a surprise."

"Then how come you know about it?" Connor asked.

Nate grinned. "The AI doesn't know how to keep a secret," he explained. "She--I mean, *it*--reminded my Mom about the drill and the prize assembly when I happened to be in the kitchen this morning."

He pulled a pencil out of his hair and started writing his thank you note. Then he added, "Mom says that's okay because we have no secrets in our family. But she really meant she doesn't want *Dad and me* to have secrets. It messes with her ability to run everything."

Nate must have been right about the drill being today because Teresa made a special trip across the room to warn us.

"You boys better be on your best behavior today," she said, looming over Ryan's desk. "I don't want my mom, I mean the school, to look bad in front of the special visitors."

Apparently, there are no secrets in Teresa's house either.

"Don't worry, Teresa," scoffed Ryan. "We know all about the "special visitors", and I have a plan to show them what we're made of."

For some reason, this didn't seem to reassure her. Teresa frowned and flounced back to her side of the room. Maybe she didn't want to give credit to anyone but her mom for protecting the school.

After she left, Ryan bragged: "I've been analyzing all the astronauts' mistakes on *Zombie Bash III: Space Station Offensive*. Defending the school ought to be pretty much the same as defending a space station," he asserted. "In fact, it'll be easier because the shooter won't be undead!"

"Do you think the teachers know about the surprise drill?" I wondered.

"Let's find out," said Deven. "Mr. Isaak?" he said, raising his voice, "is there an assembly this afternoon?"

Mr. Isaak didn't bother to glance at the calendar on his desk. "Possibly," he answered.

"Will Homeworld Security be there?" Ryan asked.

Mr. Isaak looked up and blinked.

"He means Home*land* Security," I explained.

"He's been playing too much *Space Police*," Connor added.

"Then perhaps these questions should be directed to our Police resource officer," said Mr. Isaak in a bored voice.

"Won't Officer Racarro be kind of busy today?" Deven asked.

"I have no idea," said Mr. Isaak. He was playing it pretty close the vest...or maybe he was really as bored as he sounded. It was hard to tell.

Actually, we hadn't seen Officer Racarro on our way in this morning. It was possible he had the day off so we'd be on our own during the drill. *He might be playing* **Space Police** *right now*, I thought jealously.

"All right, Dudes, we better get our game faces on," Ryan urged us.

"Mr. Isaak, can I watch the door?" Connor asked.

Mr. Isaak sighed. "If you can do so from your seat," the teacher answered.

So, Connor took first watch while the rest of us waited tensely for the drill to begin.

Mr. Isaak watched Connor watching the door with a frown on his face for the first thirty seconds. Then he focused on drinking his coffee.

I tried to focus on my thank you note:

> Dear Sarge,
> Thank you for teaching us a bunch of ways to hurt someone in Mr. Isaak's class.
> I have a feeling it's going to be useful pretty soon.
> Sincerely,
> Tyler

But it didn't happen in homeroom.

"You know what this means, guys," said Ryan during the passing period.

"Mr. Isaak's going to need more coffee?" I guessed.

"The drill is going to come when we're least expecting it!" Ryan explained. Luckily, it turned out Ryan had been pretty much thinking about nothing else but repelling armed intruders in all of his classes for the last six weeks (which probably explains his grades).

Of course, he wasn't the only one. Teresa had been complaining about her mom getting emails and calls from parents whose children were freaked out by all the talk of violence. And I figured the parents themselves were probably freaking too, because the PTA kept sending emails about new security measures.

The important thing, though, is that Ryan wasn't scared. He was prepared.

"Logically, the drill has to come before seventh period," Nate pointed out. "The prize assembly will be at the end of the day when we usually have assemblies."

"That still leaves six possible periods to surprise us," Connor said.

"Only we're going to foil them by being ready all day," said Ryan with a fierce grin. "Just stick with me," he advised. "I have a plan for every classroom on the schedule."

The passing bell rang and we all went to class--except Connor, who went to his locker first. He figured he was going to need emergency snacks.

Mrs. Gutierrez has more patience than the Dudes, I guess, because we made it all the way to 6th period PE without any unusual danger.

"Coach Rachel is out for maternity leave," Teresa told us when she came out of the girls' locker room.

The Dudes nodded. "That explains her weight gain and lack of pep over the last few weeks," said Nate.

"Coach Gregor will be covering her classes for the rest of the year," Teresa announced. "Where is he, anyway?"

The Dudes explained that Coach Gregor liked to spend P.E. in his office in the boys' locker room, away from kids.

"Welcome to our world," said Deven, handing Teresa a bucket and a gum-scraper.

Melanie was coming back from the water fountain in the hall. "There are a bunch of people in the lobby," she said with a curious look on her face and water on her chin.

"Who?" Teresa asked.

Melanie shrugged. "Adults," she said, like they all look alike.

"Are they armed?" Connor asked.

Melanie swallowed as if her mouth was dry again already. "Um, one guy had a camera," she said.

Ryan's eyes gleamed. "They must have brought in a committee of observers to judge our preparedness. We can expect an attack any minute."

"What?!" gasped Teresa.

"It's happening! It's happening!" screeched Deven excitedly.

Ryan handed his scraper to Melanie. "Better keep this," he said. "You're going to need a weapon." Then he turned to me. "Secure those doors," he said.

Girls were still trickling out of the girls' locker room. I hastily waved them through into the gym and closed the double doors. Like Sarge had taught us, I covered the door windows with health posters so the intruder couldn't see in. I didn't have Coach Gregor's key, so I got his dust-mop instead and slid the handle through the handles of the double doors.

"All right, everybody, listen up," Ryan said in his command voice. "We're facing an emergency lock-down situation and we're in the hot zone," he announced.

"What?" Teresa protested. "But that's..."

"Follow my orders exactly if you want to live!" Ryan commanded, drowning her out. Then he swung into action.

"Connor," he said, "ammo up!"

"Tyler, mine the enemy's approach!"

"Nate, we need cover," he said.

"Deven, help Nate, and be ready to use your psychological warfare effects."

"Yes sir!" said Deven with a salute.

"Wait a minute," argued Teresa. "If this is an attack, shouldn't we evacuate?"

"Good thinking, Teresa!" said Ryan, taking the path of least resistance. "You take the fire exit and lead the rest of the class to the rendezvous point. The Dudes will fight a holding action until you're safe."

Ryan had figured it just right. There was no way Teresa was going to refuse to lead the class, so, in no time, the gym was empty of everyone but the Dudes.

In front of the door, I scattered hula hoops and hand weights on the ground to trip the bad guy, or at least make it hard to advance without looking down. Ryan helped me move the badminton nets to funnel access so the bad guy couldn't flank us. Then he handed out rackets to each of the Dudes.

In the gym, we were lacking in staplers, scissors, and magazines. However, Connor found all the bins of balls: playground balls, volley balls, tennis balls, basketballs, even badminton birdies. He lined them up behind the barbican Nate was building out of gym locker baskets. The sweaty clothes were unlikely to stop a bullet, but the smell might offer some defense.

Nate also figured out how to lower and raise the basketball hoop so he could tie on a tetherball to be kind of a swinging-mace defense.

I was watching him when the doors suddenly rattled behind me.

"They're here!" I hissed, and everybody quieted down in time for me to hear someone on the other side of the door say something about "shooting in the gym" and then rattle the door again.

Nate hurriedly raised the basketball hoop into place and nodded.

"We're ready for them," said Ryan. "Unbolt the door."

I slid the dust-mop out of the door handles.

We all waited, but nothing happened.

"I hope they haven't taken their attack elsewhere," Nate said.

"Yeah," said Deven. "The other classrooms can't possibly be as ready for this drill as we are."

But the doors rattled again, and then they swung open.

It was Coach Gregor playing the bad guy with a key in his hand instead of a fake gun.

"Attack!" shouted Ryan, whacking a tennis ball. Spheres of all sizes rained down on the intruder.

If he was surprised, our assailant didn't show it. Without saying a word, the coach moved forward, blinking as balls and birdies bounced off his powerful physique. Hoops rattled and popped up under his heavy tread. Then he faltered slightly as his foot caught on a kettlebell. Looking down, Coach Gregor turned aside to avoid the kettlebell and walked right into the badminton net. The net was stretched between upright poles on stands which now fell over and dragged behind him as he turned again and moved forward like a juggernaut.

It was at that point that Nate released the tetherball, which arced toward the door but missed Coach Gregor. Instead, it knocked the hat off a woman who was behind him--the mayor! The intruder appeared to have captured the observers.

"Rescue the hostages!" yelled Ryan.

Connor and I ran forward and hustled the mayor and the other four civilians to relative safety under the bleachers.

"What's going on here?" the mayor asked me.

That would have been a great time to explain Ryan's strategy and show all we'd learned from Sarge, but, right about then, Deven got on the sound system and started his "noise that will make your eardrums break if you hear it". The observers and I covered our ears.

Meanwhile, our assailant didn't seem to notice the loss of his hostages. He continued to move toward the barricade, key extended. I'd had nightmares about this scenario. Probably we all had this year. (Except Nate. He tends to dream about robots.)

Luckily, Ryan had used his nightmares to plan tactics. At the last minute, he tossed a sweaty PE shirt toward the foe, giving it a spin so that it landed on Coach Gregor's wide head and covered his eyes. With the shooter blinded, Ryan signaled for retreat, and the Dudes sprinted past the coach and out the door to safety.

We ran the whole two blocks to the Starbucks, where we found the rest of the class. (It was probably the most exercise we had gotten all year in P.E.) As we walked in the door, we found a room full of kids in P.E. shorts and Teresa negotiating for a bulk hot-chocolate order.

Luckily, the mayor had brought along a photographer (to "shoot" pictures in the gym) as well as the Head of the Kiwanis Club, and two religious leaders (these were the hostages) so we could see how it all came out.

It turned out, that Mrs. Gutierrez had been worried about those nightmares everyone was having and the calls she was getting from parents. So, that morning, she had cancelled the security drill in favor of something more positive: A Youth Community Service Assembly. The hostages were people she had brought in, not to observe an attack but to give speeches about brotherly love and volunteering.

And they demonstrated it pretty well. The picture which ran in the Sherwood Spotlight Online showed the Imam from the local mosque coaxing the mayor out from under the bleachers while the President of the Kiwanis Club fetched her hat. And, in the foreground, Pastor Keisha shook the meaty hand of Coach Gregor, who still had a volleyball net wrapped around his shoulders.

Of course, our class missed that assembly. But Mrs. Gutierrez felt bad about how we had pelted Coach Gregor, so she pressured the PTA into giving *him* the Most Prepared Award even though there was no official drill.

The prize was a pizza party for the class--real round pizzas cooked by a restaurant, not the lunchroom--and a new rolling office chair for the coach. It better be a sturdy one!

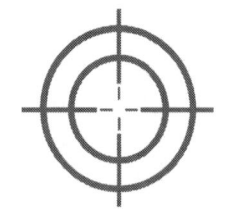

17 Dudes Upcycle

Our resource officer was back at school on Monday.

"What's up, Officer Racarro?" Deven asked. "You look kind of bummed."

Racarro sighed. "I shouldn't tell you this, but the package thieves have started up again," he said.

"Awesome!" said Connor.

"I know," said Racarro. "I really want to catch them, but I'm stuck at school."

"Us too," Deven sympathized.

"At least over winter break I was out on the streets," said the policeman. "But the perps didn't show," he complained.

"Probably because they saw your squad car," Nate reasoned. "It's actually good that you prevented crime from happening," he added.

"Sure. You saved Christmas gifts," I pointed out.

"Although, Mom says *after* Christmas is when people order what they really want. So the stakes are still pretty high," Connor said.

"They steal during the day while people are at work. So, Aziz and Morgan get to focus on the case while I'm stuck at school," Racarro said glumly.

"Cheer up," said Nate. "Maybe the package thieves will make a move on a weekend or public holiday."

Racarro nodded. "There was an uptick in package thefts again over Spring Break. By then, a bunch of residents had gotten doorbell cameras, but the thieves had started wearing masks."

"Diabolical," said Nate.

"Yeah." The policeman explained, "Because of the time stamps we know that three packages were stolen from three different houses at the same date and time."

"That means there's a whole crew of porch pirates," Connor said.

"Yeah," said Racarro. "And take a look at this," he said, pulling up a picture on his phone.

The Dudes gathered around to see an orange truck with a splotch of gray primer on the back fender. "We caught a picture of the pickup truck they use to carry their haul. Unfortunately, they had covered their license plate," the officer said.

"It's an arms race," said Connor.

"Yeah," said Ryan. "If they have a truck, you have to get a tank."

"That'd be great," agreed Racarro, but the city already spent all its money on the Mobile Emergency Command Vehicle," he lamented. "Besides, people are kind of against the police acting like the military these days. You guys don't have any new leads, do you?" he asked hopefully.

"Just that there are tater tots in the lunch room today," said Connor.

Racarro's shoulders slumped. "I hope nothing happens until school is over," he said. "Anyway, Aziz had a good idea," he went on. "She thinks maybe they'll go back to the woods to sort through their loot."

"Like in that clearing where we found all the boxes?" Connor asked.

"Yeah," said Racarro. "Morgan says we can plan a stakeout!" he said excitedly.

"Cool!" said all the Dudes.

"Can we come with you? We know how to make weapons out of magazines and staplers," Connor informed him.

Before Racarro could reply, someone cleared their throat suddenly behind us.

"Excuse me, officer," said Mrs. Gutierrez's voice. "Is there a reason you are keeping these students out of homeroom?"

Racarro jumped. "Oh, uh, no ma'am. That is,..."

"We were just helping him with an inquiry," Ryan spoke up.

"Official police business," Nate added.

"We can't comment on an active investigation," Deven put in.

"I see," said Mrs. Gutierrez, watching Racarro swallow nervously. "Well, if you're finished with them, perhaps the boys should go on to class. The bell rang ten minutes ago," she added, holding the door open for us.

"Oh, yeah, right. Uh, thank you, boys," said Officer Racarro. "And, uh, don't do drugs!" he shouted after us.

"The city really ought to buy the police a tank," Connor said that afternoon after school as he and Ryan wrestled Coach Gregor's old rolling chair onto the bus.

"An armored vehicle might be overkill against package thieves," Nate pointed out. "It's not the kind of thing that should be used on civilian criminals."

"You never know," Connor said as the bus started moving. "The mayor bought that MECC, and right away we had some emergencies."

"Then what would we have if they bought a tank," I asked, "a war?"

"Nate and Tyler are right," Ryan said. "A tank would be more useful in Dude hands. Remember how Teresa's soccer team powned us last summer? We totally need some armor the next time we face them."

There was no arguing with that, so, when the bus dropped us off, we rolled Coach Gregor's chair to my house to discuss Ryan's plan.

The dome climber was in the front yard where the Dudes had left it last week. My mom had noticed it right away when she got home from work. And the dinnertime discussion had gone like this:

"Where did that dome come from?" Mom had asked over the noise. (Now that Mamaw was gone, we had gone back to lip smacking and silverware drumming.) Her eyes had shot toward Dad, who was keeping his head down as usual so as not to be blamed for stuff he didn't hear.

"The Dudes and I got it at the Give and Take," I had explained. (This confession was strategic. I figured Mom didn't want to talk about the Give and Take because Leon's nursery was now stuffed with things she'd gotten for him there.)

She had pivoted to a new complaint instead. "It really doesn't belong in the front yard," she said. "It'll be in the way--won't it, Jason?"

In response to his name, Dad had raised his head. "Wait, there's something out front?" he asked. (His cluelessness was *not* strategic. Now that he works at home, he doesn't get out of the back yard much.)

"Don't worry," I had hastened to reassure. "We'll move it before you start mowing."

I had him there. Dad didn't want to bring up the question of when he would start mowing the yard. He tries to keep mowing season as short as possible (and the grass as long as possible.) So, he had strategically turned the discussion over to Jayden and his comparison between Ironman's suit and Batman's utility belt.

Anyway, now we had a dome *and* a battered office chair in the front yard.

"The benefits of a geodesic dome are that it is strong and encloses a large area," Nate explained.

The Dudes stood around the dome, passing a box of crackers I had snagged from the house. Well, we were all standing except Connor, who was sitting in the office chair. And we were all eating except Deven, who was spinning Connor in the chair fast enough to spray cracker crumbs every time Connor took a bite.

"We could have used something like this to protect us from Teresa's soccer bombs last summer," I pointed out, taking another step away from Connor. "The tents totally didn't cut it."

The Dudes shuddered at the memory of the whole girls' team sending a hail of soccer balls from Teresa's yard into mine.

"But wouldn't the balls go between the bars and smash us?" asked Deven, stopping the chair and watching Connor fall off in the grass.

"That's why we need to attach armor plating," said Ryan logically.

Luckily, the rain had finally stopped about mid-May, so we could safely haul the cardboard boxes out of the basement. And when Connor stopped weaving all over the yard with dizziness, Ryan sent him home to get a Warehouse Store 10-pack of duct tape.

We separated the flattened boxes by size and started taping them to the bars of the climber. Bigger boxes--like would hold Rob's 20lb. bags of dog food--covered the triangle spaces just right. We overlapped smaller boxes around specialty cut-outs like for the periscope (the one Nate made for Grandad's RV on our camping trip last summer). We also attached a long wrapping paper tube to be a 90mm gun barrel. (It was just for show, of course. The real fire power would have to come from our dart guns.)

Meanwhile, Nate sketched out a way to attach the structure to our bikes so that it could roll rather than having to be carried.

"It would be better with tracks," Ryan remarked, "but Dad says he can't afford *one* snowmobile, much less two!"

So, it would be a wheeled tank. Jayden's wagon and Coach Gregor's old rolling chair would support the weight. And Nate would attach two bicycles to provide power and maneuverability:

"Maneuvering an armored vehicle of this scale will require practice," Nate warned us.

"Dudes! Fall in for motorized vehicle drill!" Ryan commanded.

We tried it first on our feet. The wide-open space of the cul-de-sac was the perfect place to practice. Since Connor and I were to be the left and right tracks (we had the sturdiest bikes), Nate had us hold each end of a broom to simulate being connected to the tank. It wasn't easy. To go straight Connor and I had to move at the same speed. To turn left, I had to speed up while Connor slowed down. To turn right, I had to slow down and let Connor speed up.

Of course, once we were inside the tank, we would have to pedal in synch without being able to see where we were going. To practice this, we put on blindfolds and listened to directions from Nate (who would be using the tank's periscope when the time came).

About the time we were beginning to get the hang of it, Mrs. Kostenko came home from her job at the craft store.

She drove up quietly in her electric car and watched us for a good ten minutes before we realized we had an audience.

She must have thought we were practicing for marching band because, when we saw her, she said, "I can't wait for football season."

This was weird, because it was June. But the Dudes are always polite, so we just nodded and smiled the way we always did when adults brought up random topics.

Mrs. Kostenko pulled the car into her driveway and plugged-in then walked back down the yard to talk to us.

"Memorial Day is coming up, you know," she said.

The Dudes nodded and smiled again.

"Maybe you boys could do a performance for the block party," she suggested.

"Uh, I don't know..." I started to say.

But Ryan was all over that. "We'd be *happy* to provide a show of force--I mean to show off our maneuvers," he told her.

"And what's this?" she asked, gesturing toward the cardboard covered dome, "A float?"

"You guessed it!" said Ryan as Deven said "Huh?"

Then Ryan frowned. "The only problem is we need a place to park it that's off the grass."

"Ooh! How creative," gushed Mrs. Kostenko. "You can park it in the cul-de-sac. I'll call all the neighbors and let them know about your special project so they don't make a complaint," she promised. "It will generate buzz for the Memorial Day Block Party too," she added.

"Perfect," said Ryan with a wave. Then he signaled for the four of us to help him lift the tank-in-progress and carry it into the street.

"Now we're doing a performance?" I complained when Mrs. Kostenko had gone inside.

"Don't worry, Tyler," Ryan said as we set the dome onto the pavement. "At least now your dad can mow the grass."

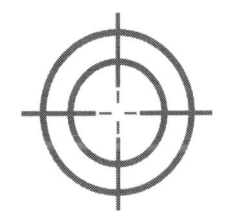

18 Dudes Tank the Neighborhood

Connor and I, as the tracks, were the most important part of our armored vehicle. When we had mastered walking, we attached the broomstick between our bikes and practiced pedaling in sync without falling off. Deven made an Ultimate Tank Boogie Mix to help us keep the rhythm.

We all practiced on our own too. It was lucky we were so close to the end of the school year. (Otherwise, the hour a day of playing *Trax Campaign* online would have eaten into homework time.)

As Mrs. Kostenko had promised, no one complained about us keeping a tank in the cul-de-sac. This was only fair. After all, Mr. Ramirez down the street always had a car under a tarp in front of his house.

Ryan and Connor brought a tarp to cover our tank too in case of rain. The tarp had a smiling seal painted on it. Covering the dome, he looked like he had a secret. I knew he had more than one. It wasn't the first time he'd covered a Dude project.

On Saturdays, Mr. Ramirez would remove his tarp (which had nothing painted on it) to reveal a Pontiac GTO. Then he would get under the car and do something--changing the oil, maybe. (Teresa went over there once to make sure he knew about Sherwood's oil recycling program to protect the salmon spawning streams from dumped oil. Our tank was 100% recycled components, but I still hoped Teresa wouldn't come nosing around.)

The next Saturday it was dry and sunny. The Dudes came over to work on the tank. Nate had figured how to screw a cross-beam onto the frames of Connors bike and mine, using those holes where you can attach a water bottle holder. Then he attached the dome to the cross beam where it wouldn't interfere with pedaling. Except when we had to hold the dome for him, the rest of us mostly stood around talking.

Down the street, Mr. Ramirez's friends were doing the same thing while Mr. Ramirez's feet stuck out from under the GTO. Sometimes they would pass him a wrench or one of the sandwiches that Mrs. Ramirez had brought out on a tray.

Mom didn't bring the Dudes sandwiches. It probably takes a while to work out a routine like that, and the Dudes weren't planning to work on the tank for the rest of our lives. We basically had two weeks to get operational before the Memorial Day Block Party.

We had finished attaching the cardboard armor. But there was a lot of work to do on the inside. As I've said, my bike and Connor's would be the wheels/tracks. The Elephant gun, attached to its tripod gun mount, would ride in Jayden's wagon, which was also holding up the front end of the dome. Connor had adjusted Coach Gregor's old rolling office chair to the height we needed to support the back end of the tank and strapped it on with some of his dad's old belts.

Ryan would be our **unit commander and gunner**. He would walk behind the wagon, protected inside the tank, and fire the Elephant Gun straight ahead through a flap in the tank's armor. Of course, he only had three effective shots unless we managed to recover any ammo on mission. So, we were somewhat limited in fire-power.

To make up for this, Deven would carry his Alpha Squad Destroyer and wear his grandmother's gardening belt to carry ammo. Since we didn't have a rotating turret (Nate was already working on a redesign), we cut flaps all around the vehicle. As **loader**, Deven would have the most mobility inside the tank to fire from the flaps and also to pick up any darts we happened to run over.

Nate would walk at the center of the dome and use the periscope. When the tank was in motion, he would call out orders to the **driver** and **co-driver** (that's Connor and me) just like a real tank **commander**. Luckily, once we attached the tank to the bikes, the dome was lifted a couple feet so that Connor and I only had to hunch a little when we pedaled and the other guys could mostly stand up all the time.

To complete the illusion, we had a Bluetooth speaker for sound effects. It was round, and Deven had mounted it inside the fake gun tube to magnify and direct the noise. He had made a recording of the sound of tanks crashing through bushes and shooting Nazis and stuff.

"I got it off the Streaming History Channel," he told us. "It's basically all Nazis and mega-weapons--you know, history for guys who like watching videos. It's my favorite channel after Wacky Cat Views."

The last thing we did was spray the outside of the tank with the green and gray paint I got at the Give and Take. Along with the brown of the cardboard, it made great camo and helped cover some of the logos on the boxes.

On the night of the Memorial Day Welcome Summer Block Party, the Dudes weren't enjoying the barbecue and lemonade. We were busy putting the finishing touches on the tank, while my dad loitered nearby, holding a hot dog.

I knew why. Ever since fourth grade, when we went on ninja maneuvers during a Memorial Day Block Party and came home in our underwear, our parents have been especially concerned to keep us in sight on that night. Apparently, it was Dad's assignment this year, so I was surprised when I saw Mom approaching with my little brothers in tow.

Leon was toddling beside her, clinging to her finger with one hand and waving a little American flag with the other. The VFW gives those little flags away when you donate, and Mom always donates on Memorial Day. Jayden also had a flag, so I guess either she donated twice or the VFW decided to prevent a war on the home front.

(In case you didn't know, VFW doesn't stand for any bad words. It means: Veterans of Foreign Wars.)

As Mom walked up, Dad anxiously reported: "They're still here." He gestured toward the Dudes with his hot dog so mustard and relish dripped on the grass.

Mom cast her gaze over the tank. I guess it was the first time she'd seen it with the tarp off. "Did you ask them about all the camouflage and guns and things?" she asked Dad.

Dad frowned. "You said to keep an eye on them, so I kept an eye on them," he said, defensively. He started stuffing his hot dog in his mouth, so Mom turned to me.

"Tyler?" she said. "I thought you boys were making a float."

"It's a tank, Mom," I told her.

"Cool!" shrieked Jayden. He immediately dropped to his belly on the pavement to peer underneath.

"Actually, it's an armored vehicle," explained Nate, but Mom was shaking her head.

"You can't use this tonight!" she sputtered, nearly pulling Leon off his feet as she tried to cross her arms.

"Seriously?" I said. "We've been working on it for two weeks."

She turned a concerned frown on Dad. "Did you know about this?" she asked.

Luckily, Dad had just finished swallowing his hot dog. "How could I know what was happening all the way in the front yard?" he replied.

Mom rolled her eyes. "With all the unrest in America's cities right now, the boys can't enact using a military vehicle to terrorize civilians!" she hissed. "No one wants to be reminded of politics on Memorial Day."

"Don't worry, Mrs. Reynolds, we only want to terrorize girls," Ryan pointed out.

"That's even worse!" Mom cried. "This is supposed to be a friendly neighborhood gathering. We can't have you starting a riot...or a hashtag!"

I hadn't seen any unrest in Sherwood, though the adults had been kind of tense lately, especially when they watched the news.

Speaking of tense, just then, Mrs. Kostenko came over, looking at her watch.

Mom and Dad froze in the face of her cheery grin.

"It'll be time for fireworks soon," Mrs. Kostenko informed us. "Well?" she asked briskly, looking around. Her gaze caught on Jayden's legs sticking out from under the tank, just like Mr. Ramirez under his car. "Are we ready?" she asked.

"Give us five minutes," Ryan said quickly. He whispered something to Deven and Connor and sent them running home. Then he turned to my Mom. "Don't worry, Mrs. Reynolds. We can make the tank into a festive non-controversial float."

Mrs. Kostenko had roped off an area in the center of the cul-de-sac for our performance. Being a crafting professional, she had used red, white and blue crepe paper so it wouldn't look like crime scene tape. There were already kids lining the tape, ready for our parade.

I dragged Jayden out from under the edge of the tank and sent him to the viewing area. Then I crawled under and got on my bike, Nate set up his periscope, and Ryan checked that the gun carriage was ready to roll.

Meanwhile, Connor and Deven came running back, and I saw their sneakers moving around the tank before they too scrambled underneath and into position.

"All right, Team," said Ryan. "You know our mission: Deploy for Operation Friendly Freedom!"

When Nate barked "MOVE OUT" Connor and I started pedaling. (Ryan put his hands on the Elephant Gun to steady it, but he didn't plan to fire during the parade.)

Nate peered through the periscope and ordered: "HARD RIGHT SLOW". Connor and I swung the tank wide out of its parking space and toward the center of the cul-de-sac where dozens of little kids lined the performance area.

How do you make a tank less militaristic? Deven had draped the rainbow-colored parachute he got at the Give and Take over the top to cover the camouflage. Connor had brought his stash of candy too, which he had dumped into Deven's ammo belt. At the last minute, Ryan remembered to order Deven to turn off the sounds of Nazi devastation.

Luckily, Deven had discovered some amazing music on Wacky Cat Views. It's not music about cats or for cats. It's music made *by* cats (with some human collaboration, I guess). So, as we rolled forward then turned in a circle for the crowd, wacky cat music filled the air and Deven threw candy out the gunports.

The crowd loved it! Afterwards, everyone shared their cell-phone photos online. And the Sherwood Spotlight reported that the neighborhood's "Pride display" was well-received. Turns out weapons of war are anti-personnel by nature, whereas Pride floats are, um, *for* personnel, I guess.

Anyway, our message was a little garbled. In our minds, it was a message of deterrence: "Watch out! We have a mega-weapon." And that message was only meant for Teresa!

19 Dudes Make Tracks

We had never talked about what we would do after the show, but of course, we had to get the tank out of the center of the cul-de-sac so people could sit there to watch the fireworks. Besides, we had run out of candy, and we didn't want to start a riot of little kids. The thing is, we couldn't just back up to our parking place at the curb because bikes can't go backwards. The only thing to do was head off down the street.

Right away I found out that practicing with the broomstick hadn't prepared me for what it would be like to ride my bike with no view of what was ahead. If Connor and I hadn't had absolute faith in our leaders, it never would have worked.

It was dark inside the tank--I mean really dark. Remember, it was dark outside, and we had a layer of cardboard armor over us and rainbow nylon layered over that.

"The tank is too wide to make a U-turn on Sherwood Court," Nate pointed out.

"We're going to have to circle the block," decided Ryan.

"AHEAD SLOW" Nate ordered.

Of course, Sherwood Heights is in the suburbs. So, there were no real blocks. A lot of streets didn't even go through (hence the cul-de-sacs) and, even when they did, they created more of a long, distorted trapezoid than a block. It might take us a while to get back to the block party.

And this is where we ran into trouble with Nate, because, even though he is great at commanding which track to move to get us turned the right way, he doesn't have a map in his head. The periscope prevented him from seeing the sky too, so celestial navigation was out.

Another problem was that we had more than one leader. Nate was calling out steering directions. But Ryan was peering through the front gunport and calling out stuff too.

"Dog at two-o-clock!" shouted Ryan. "That's a friendly. Little Free Library at eleven-o-clock!"

He squeezed off a couple rounds.

"Direct hit on a parked car at three-o-clock!" he reported. "Now we need to retrieve ammo."

"PIVOT RIGHT" Nate commanded in response.

Deven turned on the flashlight app on his phone so Ryan could see to snatch the Elephant darts off the ground.

"EASE BACK. PIVOT LEFT. FORWARD SPEED," Nate ordered.

"This is awesome," Ryan crowed, as Connor and I pedaled the tank back to the middle of the road. It wasn't hard. Since we were headed downhill, Connor and I actually had to ride the brakes. You see, Nate and Ryan had to walk along with us while using the periscope and the Elephant Gun respectively. At the same time, Deven was side-stepping around them while zig-zagging from one gunport to another. This took real coordination. (It's a good thing he had so much practice with the chicken dance!)

"Uh, guys?" Deven said suddenly. "Do you get the feeling we're being watched?"

Now that he mentioned it, I couldn't help noticing an eerie feeling that conflicted with the happy music.

"Check our six!" Ryan commanded.

"Deven looked out the gunport in back and shouted, "Car!" It must have snuck up on us. Now that Deven mentioned it, I could see the glow of headlights shining in from under the back edge of the tank.

Connor and I stopped pedaling and waited for orders. I mean, when somebody yells "Car!" you're supposed to get off the street. That's the kids' code of safety. But the tank didn't have anywhere to go. It was way too big for the bike lane or the sidewalk. And Nate said our connections (made mostly of duct tape) weren't stable enough to risk riding with one track up on the curb.

"We have to get out of the way," I said.

Ryan peered through the front gunport. "Turn left onto Sherwood Drive," he shouted.

"HARD LEFT!" ordered Nate immediately.

I stood on the pedals while Connor took his time. Ryan jammed the wagon's handle to the right to swivel the wheels left, and the rollers on Coach Gregor's old chair rattled as the tank swung in a wide arc onto Sherwood

Drive. I heard the rev of a motor as the car behind us sped off down Sherwood Lane.

We made it! This street was quiet, and, in another hundred yards, we made another left onto Sherwood Heights Road, headed up the hill.

Normally, from here we would have used the No Man's Land trail to cut through to Country Club Lane and then back to my street. And it would have been awesome to smash through, pushing down trees! But, of course, we weren't in a real tank. So, we were going to have to take the long way up Sherwood Heights Road past the high school and the Retirement Community to where Country Club Drive crossed. That was a lot of pedaling--and all uphill.

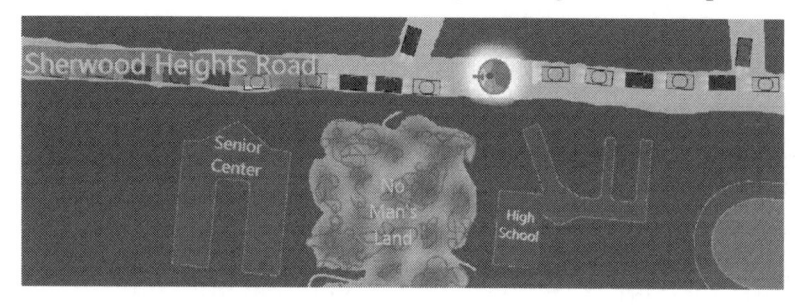

Usually, Sherwood Heights Road is the toughest hill the Dudes ever take on our bikes. Still, with a little huffing and puffing, we always make it without stopping. This time, Connor and I immediately noticed how much harder it was to pedal uphill with half the weight of a tank on your bike.

Also, Sherwood Heights Road is what they call an arterial. That means it's the road that everyone has to use if they want to get from downtown Sherwood, at the bottom of the hill, to the Sherwood Heights neighborhoods at the top and then down the other side to the Sammammish Valley neighborhoods beyond.

"Car!" yelled Deven again.

And this is where that arterial thing became a problem.

"Car!"

Because people were driving up the hill...

"Car!"

...to Sherwood Heights and getting stuck behind a slow-moving, tank.

"Okay, one of the cars is turning off," Deven announced. "He's trying to find a way around us."

"There isn't one," said Ryan, who *did* have a map in his head. "All the turn-offs are dead ends."

"Yep, he's made a u-turn in Robin Hood Circle and is coming back," Deven reported a minute later. "Only he can't get back onto Sherwood Heights Road because nobody is letting him in."

I didn't say anything, because I didn't have the breath. Connor and I were panting and sweating, but the tank was moving slower and slower.

"I have an idea," said Ryan. He ran to the left gunport and stuck his arm out. "I'll signal them to go around," he said.

"It's working!" Deven shouted from our six. "The car behind us is pulling into the left lane and the others are following. They're going to pass us!" he said.

But he spoke too soon.

We heard the rev of a car beside us, then the screech of brakes followed by what sounded like a dozen horns mingling with the yowls from Deven's speaker.

"Uh-oh," said Nate, peering into the periscope. "There were cars coming the other way," he explained. "There's a truck parked beside the road, and nobody can see around it. They're backed up past the next intersection now," he announced. "It looks like we're in gridlock."

"Hey! I see lights," said Deven from the rear gunport. "Have the fireworks started?"

But they hadn't. The lights were on the top of a police car, and they were coming up the hill. As Deven watched, the squad car pulled up on the curb way back by the high school and parked. Then Officer Racarro came running uphill to the center of the traffic jam (which was us, of course).

When he reached us, he stood panting, staring at our rainbow-draped dome while wacky cat music filled the air. He jumped when the front gunport flipped open and Ryan yelled, "Hi, Officer Racarro! How come you're not at the stakeout?"

Through the gunport, I could see Racarro panting. He ran his hand through his hair. "Morgan sent me to find out what all the horns are about," he said, glancing around nervously, and coughing a little. I couldn't blame him. The exhaust was getting to me too. (I hope when you future dudes are reading this, all the cars are electric.)

"This, um, vehicle is a problem," Racarro said. "You're too slow, and you don't have lights."

"I can fix that," said Deven, pushing a button on his phone for "Disco Mode". Pulsing lights filled the tank and flashed from under the edges and out the gunports.

"You're holding up traffic," Racarro shouted over the noise of honking cars.

"We know!" yelled Connor.

"Are you going to give us a ticket?" Ryan asked.

"I'm going to get you out of the road," Racarro decided. He looked around. To the right of the road was a solid line of backyard fences. To the left was the sidewalk and a strip of mowed grass about ten feet wide between the street and the trees of No Man's Land.

Racarro strode into the left lane and signaled the cars to back up a little and make room.

"He's motioning us toward him," Ryan reported.

"MOVE OUT. HARD LEFT. SLOW," Nate ordered.

Racarro backed away as we followed, cutting across the left lane. Then he helped lift as we bumped up over the curb into the grass.

At last, we were out of traffic. Behind us, on Sherwood Heights Road, cars pulled back into their proper lanes and started to move in both directions--all except the truck that was still parked at the side of the road.

"Hey," said Ryan, peering out the right gunport. "Isn't that the truck owned by the package thieves?"

"What?" said Racarro, running around the side of the tank to see.

"Confirmed," Nate said from the periscope. "I recognize the spot of gray primer over the bumper."

Connor and I hopped off our bikes and joined Ryan at the side gunport. The truck was parked on the street, but there were no bad guys inside.

"They must be in the forest getting the loot!" said Deven excitedly.

"They're supposed to come out on Sherwood Lane," said Racarro. "That's where the stakeout is!"

"But their getaway vehicle is here," Connor pointed out.

Just then, Nate shouted: "Insurgents at 12 o'clock!"

I ran to a front gunport to see two guys in ski masks come running out of the forest. One of them was carrying a couple of pillow cases full of stuff. He skidded to a stop when he saw a pulsing, glowing rainbow tank between him and the getaway truck.

The other guy was carrying a wide flat box with a picture of a flatscreen TV on it. He couldn't see anything, I guess, and smacked right into the tank, falling backward with the flat box on top of him.

"Hold it right there!" shouted Ryan through the gunport. He cocked the Elephant Gun menacingly, although he couldn't actually aim it far enough down to cover the guy on the ground.

The standing guy dropped his loot and pulled off his mask to get a better look, which is when I found out this *guy* was a girl. (From the look in her eyes as she took in the flashing, meowing tank, I'm guessing she was probably re-thinking her decision to take drugs.)

About that time, Officer Aziz came running out of the woods, her eyes on the perp.

"Police! Stop right there!" she shouted, skidding to avoid a collision with her quarry. Aziz slapped the cuffs on the standing thief. Racarro moved quickly to uncover the flatscreen guy and arrest him too.

Deven's wacky cat music ended with a synthesized "mew". And then the fireworks started.

To her credit, Aziz didn't give the tank a second look as she radioed for back up. The Dudes cheered as she read the package thieves their rights. But Officer Morgan, who drove up in the squad car a minute later (I guess he was the backup), got out and circled our vehicle. He took his cap off and rubbed his face.

"Okay, boys," said Officer Morgan wearily. "The police action is over. Don't you think you'd better go home now?" (I don't know how he knew we were boys in there. Just a lucky guess, I suppose.)

That's when Nate spoke up. "The problem is, we can't back up and we don't have room to turn because of the trees," he explained.

Morgan scratched his head. "Racarro--you're the school Resource Officer," said Morgan. "Why don't *you* help them figure it out?"

"Yes sir," said Racarro, looking longingly at the perps who were being walked to the squad car by Officer Aziz.

He helped us lift the tank and the bikes and carry it away from the trees and back out into the street.

In the meantime, he told us how Officer Morgan had ordered a flat screen TV with police money and had it delivered to his house, knowing the thieves wouldn't be able to resist it and also that it would be hard to carry.

"We have a video of them wearing masks and taking the TV earlier today," Racarro explained.

"And now you have them in possession of the loot and the masks," Nate put in.

"Glad to be of help," said Ryan, shaking Racarro's hand through the gunport. "Well, see you around."

"Wait a minute," said the policeman. "This vehicle is not street legal," he pointed out.

"Then how are we supposed to get it home?" I asked.

Officer Racarro sighed. "I guess I'll have to give you a police escort," he said. "I'll get my car. Then you can follow me. I have a pretty good idea where you're going."

The fireworks had just ended, and people were standing up and folding their blankets when the police car showed up in Sherwood Court with its lights flashing and leading the rainbow tank.

Everyone cheered and whistled. It almost felt like we Dudes got the recognition we deserved. All the same, we didn't feel the need to explain the details to our parents.

Officer Racarro got a hot dog and a chance to hand out more See Something Say Something magnets. I figure his appearance in our impromptu parade (which was soon shared in videos and selfies on social media) did more to help Sherwood PD win the community policing award than being Resource Officer *or* catching the package thieves.

At last, the Dudes snagged some hot dogs and drinks. We had earned it. Driving an armored vehicle is hard work. Good thing we had a whole summer ahead of us. The Dudes needed to rest up before we'd be ready to take the blitzkrieg to Teresa.

THE END

Thanks for reading! If you enjoyed this book, please send the Dudes some love with a review at your favorite retailer.

Don't Miss the Next Exciting Adventure of the Dudes...

Dudes on Lock Down:

Sweatpants proliferation? Zoom-bombing grandparents? Pandemic Pets? Sherwood Heights has all the signs of a true dystopia. Luckily, the Dudes are ready to fill the power vacuum. See how the Dudes take on:

Screentime Bonanza
Socially Distanced Pest Control
Popping Pandemic Bubbles, and
Mandatory Family Game Night!

Dudes face the desperation of a community sanitizer shortage, Diwali inferno, and a DIY plunge pool—emphasis on the "plunge".

Don't miss the madness in:
DUDES DYSTOPIA

In paperback, ebook, and audiobook.

Tyler Reynolds has been entrusted with the awesome duty of preserving the legend of the Dudes' epic adventures for all time. He lives with his mom and dad, two brothers, and a dog named Rob. He spends his non-screen-time with his four best friends, and his school is a hard target.

Find his website at **thedudeschronicles.com**

Emily Kay Johnson occasionally comes out of hiding to collaborate with Tyler on the dubious project of sharing the exploits of the Dudes with the world. She lives with her husband, kids, and cats in the Pacific Northwest. She has helped recycle many boxes into mega-weapons.

You can reach her at **epicspielpress.com**

*Please remember to leave a review
at your favorite retailer!*

Made in the USA
Las Vegas, NV
31 October 2025

539a5eb9-bea0-44eb-b4ae-6a67ebc79575R01